Books by Jean Little

MINE FOR KEEPS

HOME FROM FAR

Home from Far

Home from Far

by Jean Little

Illustrated by Jerry Lazare

LITTLE, BROWN AND COMPANY
Boston   Toronto

Published simultaneously in Canada
by Little, Brown & Company (Canada) Limited

PRINTED IN THE UNITED STATES OF AMERICA

For Mother

with love

Contents

Home from Far

1

His Name Is Michael

JENNY was brushing Fleet. He lay on his side, stretching out his long legs blissfully as the wire bristles combed through his white and russet coat. He was a big dog, even for an English setter, and Jenny's arm was beginning to ache. She paused for a moment, almost giving up, but the feathers on his back and legs and his sweeping plume of a tail still needed grooming. Jenny sighed and started on them. The brush caught in a tangle on his hind leg. Impatiently, Jenny tried to jerk it through. Fleet raised his head and looked at her sadly.

"I'm sorry, boy," she said, laying the brush down on the floor beside her and flexing her right arm to take the kinks out of it.

The trouble was it had been Michael's job to brush Fleet. And to Michael it had been not a chore but a joy. Night after night, right after supper, Michael would go to the cupboard where Fleet's brush was kept. Night after night, Fleet, knowing what was coming, would prance around swooshing his great tail and getting in the boy's way. And then the two of them would settle down and talk to each other.

"But I'm not Michael," Jenny admitted. Fleet could consider himself lucky if he was brushed once a week now. And Jenny never talked. There was too much work to do, too many snarls to untangle, too much dog to cover. Of course,

Michael would never let the snarls get so bad. Jenny leaned forward.

"Where's Michael, Fleet?" she asked softly.

Fleet's head came up quickly and his tail thudded against the floor. Jenny was sorry at once. She took his eager face between her hands and rubbed his silky ears.

"It's all right, old boy. I won't talk about him any more," she promised.

Fleet was supposed to be a family dog, but he had always been Michael's since the day Dad bought him. Now he was looking at the door, but he did not get up. He had learned, just as she was still learning, that it was no use expecting Michael to walk in.

Jenny reached for the brush and Fleet shifted suddenly. He drew his gangly legs in under him and rested his chin on his paws. He looked as though he were going to sleep, but Jenny saw that he had not yet stopped watching the door.

Then, without warning, Jenny found herself living over again the nightmare afternoon when Michael was killed.

It was the last day of the Christmas holidays. Mac was spending the afternoon at a birthday party. Dad was working. The rest of them were coming home from the shopping center, where they had spent their Christmas money while Mother bought groceries. Michael was sitting up front with Mother; Jenny and Alec were riding in the back. They took turns riding in the front seat. (What if it had been her turn instead of Michael's that afternoon?) Alec was reading a comic book, whispering the words to himself as he went along. She and Mother and Michael were singing "My Grandfather's Clock."

Sitting on the kitchen floor, remembering, Jenny saw the

big Buick skid across the icy street and heard again their song falter into sudden silence. Fear clutched at the pit of her stomach, just as it had on that winter afternoon, six months ago, when she had realized that the car plunging toward them would not be able to stop in time.

Then, she was in a snowbank at the side of the road. Alec, still clutching his comic book, was sprawled beside her. They had been thrown clear through the back door.

But Mother and Michael were still in the car. Jenny stood up shakily and stared at what had been their green Plymouth. Without thinking about what she was doing, she moved forward and picked up Mother's change purse and a tin of salmon which were lying in the road. People came running. Someone pulled her back. Behind her, she heard Alec beginning to cry. Some men went to the other side of the car and managed to pry Mother's door open. A police car arrived. She saw Mother being lifted out. There was blood on her face. They put her into an ambulance. Jenny wanted to run to her, to shake her awake and hear her speak, to be comforted — but she stayed where she was.

Then, before Jenny had seen Michael, a stout lady, still wearing an apron but with a fur coat thrown over her shoulders, hustled her and Alec into a nearby house. Another lady made Jenny take two aspirin. Both children were given cups of tea. Neither of them had tasted tea before and neither of them liked it, but they drank it without complaining. It was like having to drink a whole cup of medicine, Jenny thought dully. It was all part of the queer unreal afternoon. She never saw Michael again.

They had been twins. Back in the present, with the June sunshine spilling in through the window over the sink and making bright squares on the green tile near her, Jenny felt, not for the first time, the strangeness of that fact. She and Michael had quarreled often.

"As different as chalk and cheese," Mother had said about them.

But they had had the same thin face, the same greenish eyes, the same dark brown hair. They had started school on the same day. They had celebrated one birthday instead of two. He had been like another part of herself. And then, in one afternoon, she was not "one of the Macgregor twins" any longer. She was just a girl with two younger brothers.

They had lived through the rest of the winter without him, and then through the spring. "But I am not used to it either," Jenny told Fleet.

The setter was not listening. He lay and waited quietly. Jenny got up and carried his brush to the cupboard. "I'll finish later," she told the part of herself which was remembering the tangles she had left in his coat.

The back door opened.

"Hi, Jenny," Mother said.

Jenny looked at her. There was still a scar on her forehead and another on one side of her nose. They looked like smudges of ink. Otherwise, Jenny could find no change in her face. There was nothing in her matter-of-fact voice, nothing in the blue eyes meeting Jenny's steadily, that said, "I remember Michael. I miss him all day long." And somehow, Jenny could not test Mother, as she had tested Fleet.

"Hi," she answered now, closing the cupboard door. "Is there anything for me to carry in?"

"No, thanks. I have it all here." Mother put a mound of packages down on the table. She began sorting through them, putting buns in the bread box, a new paring knife by the sink ready to be washed, a head of lettuce in the crisper. Then, stopping before she was half done, Mother stood and gazed at Jenny for a moment. Her face was as serious, her eyes as questioning, as Jenny's own had been a few seconds earlier.

"Jenny . . ." she began.

"What is it?" Jenny asked when no more words came.

"It's a secret. I thought perhaps I should tell you first, but it wouldn't be fair." Mother gave her an apologetic smile. "You'll know all about it at suppertime."

"You shouldn't start if you aren't going to finish," Jenny protested. "That's mean."

"I know it is and I'm sorry. Why don't you take Fleet and walk down to the library to meet your father? That will make the time pass more quickly. By the way, where are Alec and Mac?"

"They went to the park," Jenny replied absently. It was no use guessing. Nothing she thought of seemed at all likely.

Fleet suddenly jumped up and galloped off down the hall.

Jenny trailed after Mother to the door. Even before Mother got it open, they both heard Mac.

Alec was at the end of their front walk, dragging his younger brother along by the arm. Alec, who was nine, felt wholly responsible for Mac, who was only six.

"I'm warning you, Mac, shut up!" he yelled fiercely, shaking him.

Mac was black from head to foot. He smelled like a freshly tarred road. He was bellowing at the top of his voice. He was obviously having a good time.

Alec looked up and saw them waiting for him. He heaved a sigh of relief.

"Hiya, Fleet," he greeted the dog bounding to meet them. "Mac fell," he called to his mother.

"I can see that." Mother looked Mac over coldly. "What a mess! Stop that racket, Malcolm, if you please. It will hurt more coming off than it did going on."

Then, all at once, she started to laugh. Jenny joined her, covering her mouth with her hand. Alec stared at the two of them, without a glimmer of amusement on his face.

"Oh, Alec, you sobersides! Look at your brother!" Mother ordered. "We should take a picture of him. Even for Malcolm Macgregor, this is a record."

Alec turned and looked at Mac. He had stopped crying and was beginning to smirk instead. Mac was always ready to clown. And right at that moment, he really looked like a clown, with tar spotting his chin, cheeks, forehead and snub nose. Alec grinned at last.

"You sure are a tar baby," he said admiringly.

Mother took Mac down to the cellar to clean him up. Alec, never far from Mac, followed close on their heels. Jenny stood alone in the hall, uncertain what to do next. Then Fleet poked his cold nose into her hand and reminded her that they were going to meet Dad.

They set off down the street, side by side, the tall graceful dog and the girl, tall for eleven but a little awkward, her shoulders hunched, her straight brown hair held back by a silver clip, her greenish eyes full of dreams.

"I wish I had a sister, Fleet," she confided.

Fleet looked sympathetic. Then he smelled an interesting bush and forgot about her. Jenny waited for him automatically, her mind busily thinking up a make-believe sister. Mother had often said that what their family needed was another girl, and before Michael's death there had even been talk of someday adopting a sister. Sometimes Jenny called her Elizabeth Mary. Sometimes she changed it to Jean Louise.

"Melissa," she murmured today. She gave a tug on the leash and Fleet came. She pictured Melissa walking on her other side. She was smaller than Jenny with a white face and huge brown eyes. Her hair was silky black and cut in bangs. Jenny had always had a hankering for bangs.

"Fleet, meet Melissa," she said.

Fleet wagged his tail politely. Suddenly, he gave a pleased bark. For one instant, Jenny really believed he saw Melissa as clearly as she did. Then she saw her father coming toward them.

"Hello, Miss Janet Macgregor," he said.

"Hello," Jenny returned.

As they walked home, she told him about Mac's tumble into the tar. Dad chuckled. They walked the last three blocks in a comfortable silence.

When they were at supper, Jenny all at once thought of Mother's secret.

"What were you going to tell us?" she wanted to know.

Mother looked at Dad.

"I forgot!" she said, her eyes wide. "How could I! Well, I've hardly seen you since you came in. It's settled, Doug. They'll be here tomorrow."

"Fine," Dad replied. "Wonderful, in fact."

"Who? Who'll be here?" Mac clamored.

"What's wonderful?" Alec put in.

"Jenny's new sister," Mother said, smiling almost shyly. Jenny lowered her fork slowly and stared at her mother.

"My . . . sister!" she echoed, not believing her ears.

"Yes, your sister. Your father and I went to the Children's Aid a long time ago and offered to take a foster child. Then . . . we had the accident and nothing was done. But I met Mrs. Carmody last week and she asked me if we were still interested. And we decided we were. We didn't tell you earlier in case it didn't work out. We didn't want to disappoint you. But it was settled today and she arrives tomorrow."

Jenny was too stunned to think of questions to ask, but the boys had half a dozen ready.

"How old is she?"

"Is she as big as Jenny?"

"Is she just a baby?"

"What's her name, Mother?"

"Where will she sleep?"

"Her name is Hilda Jackson," Mother told them. "She's Mac's age. She'll sleep in Jenny's room."

Hilda! Jenny tried to take it in. She was going to have a sister named Hilda. Not Melissa. Then she remembered Mother's first words.

"You said 'they' would come tomorrow," she turned to ask. "Who's 'they'? Is somebody going to bring her?"

"Yes, someone will bring her, but that wasn't what I meant." For the first time Mother looked uncertain.

"Your mother means that you are not just going to have a new sister. We are taking Hilda's big brother too," Dad explained. "If we had not, the children would have had to be separated."

"Whoopee! A boy!" Mac shouted.

But Dad had not finished.

"He's just a couple of months older than you are, Jenny."

"What's his name?" Alec asked.

There was a moment of silence. Then Dad reached out and took Jenny's hand in his.

"His name is Michael," he said.

2

A Sister for Jenny

"FIX that corner of the spread, Jenny," Mother said.

Jenny did as she was told. Then she straightened up and looked around the room. Her old bed had been moved up from the basement for Hilda. Mac had the twin to it, but Alec, who had slept in this one until the year before, had grown long-legged and had had to have a big bed. Jenny and Mother had put all her winter clothes into the cedar chest and that left two dresser drawers and half of the closet for Hilda.

The boy was going to have Michael's room.

Jenny turned her back on her mother suddenly. "Anything else you want?" she asked over her shoulder.

"No, run along. They should be here in about one hour."

Jenny went downstairs slowly. When she neared the bottom, she could see across the hall, through the living room door, the big front window. Her brothers were there, kneeling on the window seat, their noses against the glass, watching and waiting.

Jenny loved that window seat. When the Macgregors had first moved there just after Jenny and Michael were born, Dad had had it put in especially for Mother. Ever since she had been a small girl, brought up in rented houses with rented furniture, Mother had wanted a home of her own with a window seat in it, and before they were married Dad had promised her one. Today, Jenny did not go near it.

She stalked off down the hall and paused before the long mirror. She frowned at herself. She looked so terribly ordinary. Even her green eyes were not very green — more gray really. Maybe Hilda would be beautiful. She might even have black hair and bangs like Melissa had. But Jenny doubted it. Everybody in this family had brown hair. Alec's was the color of wet sand and Mac's was golden-brown like ripe wheat. Mother's was the same color as Mac's and Dad's was almost as dark as her own. Not one of them had even a hint of curl and Dad was going bald. It all sounded so terrible that Jenny grinned in spite of herself. Supposing Dad had had curly hair, or Alec! She could not imagine anything funnier than Alec with curls.

Her smile vanished as she remembered the boy and girl who were coming. Dragging her feet every step of the way, she went out on the veranda. Mac had given up his vigil by the living room window and was out there swooping back and forth on the swing Dad had put up for them. Jenny stood and watched him.

"Hi, Jenny," he called as he swooshed by.

"Let me have a turn."

"Okay."

Alec would have said, "I was here first," but Mac stopped the swing, slid off the plank seat and stood back.

Jenny seated herself and began swaying idly back and forth, keeping the swing moving with little taps of her feet. Mac waited for a moment. Jenny ignored him.

"If you don't want to swing, let me," he said at last.

"I'm swinging," Jenny told him shortly.

"Not really."

"Well, you just try and stop me," she taunted.

Mac trusted people until they turned on him. Then he was always surprised. He studied his sister's sullen face.

"I'm tired of swinging anyhow, so there," he said airily.

"Mac!" Alec called from somewhere inside.

Mac sped away. Jenny watched him disappear. She felt more miserable than ever. She had nobody, that was what was wrong. Alec and Mac were always together. Even when they were angry at each other, they stuck together, punching at each other and yelling threats. But without Michael, she had no one. And no strange boy, no "new sister," was going to take Michael's place either.

All at once, Jenny started the swing going as though her life depended on it. Higher and higher she flew, pumping with her whole body. She didn't hear the car drive up in front of the house.

"Jenny," Mac shouted at her, sticking his head out through the veranda door. "Come on! They're here!"

"I'm busy," she said, but he was gone. Nobody heard her.

She stopped pumping but did not drag her feet to make the swing stop. Only when it had died down by itself did she get off and wander back into the house. By the time she arrived, they were all gathered in the front hall.

Michael and Hilda were standing side by side near the door. Michael looked at though he would have turned and run if the Children's Aid Worker had not been right behind him, with her hand resting on his shoulder. He did not want to stay. He did not want to stay anywhere . . . except with Pop and Hilda in a house of their own. Since there was no chance of getting away, since, even if there had been a chance, he could not desert his sister, he faced the Macgregors squarely, his back stiff, his face blank, his eyes watchful.

He took in everything with one swift glance — Mac's wide smile of welcome, Alec's grave stare, Dad coming forward with his hand out to Hilda, Mother throwing the living room door wide and telling them to stop looking like guests. Then Jenny stepped out into the hall, and he saw a face as blank, eyes as unfriendly as his own. She looked at Hilda and her eyes widened with shock.

Michael, who had never liked Aunt Dorrie but had got along with her by keeping out of her way, all at once hated her fiercely for letting Hilda look the way she did.

"Stand up straight," he hissed at her, trying to make her presentable.

Hilda's bottom lip poked out and began to wobble. She pulled away from him a little, but she still felt too lonely to leave his side.

Mrs. Carmody was prodding them toward the living room door and Mike was wishing he had let Hilda alone when Mother changed her mind.

"Jenny, you take Hilda up and show her your room," she commanded.

"I'll take Mike up," Mac offered eagerly.

"Fine," Mrs. Carmody said heartily. "Go along, children."

Jenny, who had not yet said a word, turned obediently and led the way to the stairs. All the way up, she wondered what on earth she and Hilda would do when they were alone together. Not for the first time, she envied Mac his ease with people. She could hear him, a few steps behind her, chattering away to a Michael who was as silent as she.

But after the first moment, Jenny found that she need not have worried. Without Mike's stern eye on her, Hilda relaxed. She began to talk, and to Jenny's amazement, she stopped only long enough to breathe.

"Are you the only girl?" she began.

Jenny nodded. She though of Melissa, tiny and beautiful, with her big brown eyes and her soft black bangs. Hilda was fat. Her face was fat and her legs and arms were fat and her clothes made her look even fatter. She was dressed in a frilly pink dress that was too short and too fussy for an ordinary morning. She was blonde with hair that might have been pretty if it had been done some other way. But someone had given her a permanent. It frizzled around her face in a sort of bush. Her eyes were a pretty brown but her teeth were at the in-between stage. A front one was missing, a big new one had come in and the rest were baby teeth.

Jenny swallowed a lump in her throat and listened as Hilda talked more and more rapidly.

"I was the only girl too. At Aunt Dorrie's, I mean. She always said I was just like her very own girl. She bought me this dress just last thing before they went away. She said it was my 'going-away present.'"

"Where is your aunt now?" Jenny asked politely. She could not think of anything nice she could say about Hilda's dress.

Hilda gulped as though she too had discovered a lump in her throat. But it did not keep her from talking.

"Aunt Dorrie's not really my aunt. We just always called her Aunt Dorrie. She was our neighbor before our mother died. Then Pop paid her to have us live there. But now Uncle Evan has a job in Kirkland Lake, and we can't go there because Pop works here. We can't live with Pop either, because

Mom died and he just lives in a boardinghouse and he has to work nights lots."

For a split second, Jenny was shocked to hear Hilda speak so calmly about her mother's death. Then she realized that Hilda did not even remember the woman she called Mom. Aunt Dorrie, whoever she was, must have been taking care of the Jacksons for years.

"I had my own room at Aunt Dorrie's." Hilda looked at the two beds uncertainly. "I don't want to stay here," she blurted suddenly, her face bleak for all its roundness. "I want to go live with Aunt Dorrie. Pop could come and see me."

"Would she keep you?" Jenny asked, trying to keep the surge of hope in her heart from sounding in her voice.

"No," Hilda said miserably. "Their house is too small and Pop wants us here. Kirkland Lake is a long way away."

Jenny understood, without being told, that Hilda had had this explained to her many times but had not been able to believe it yet. Her hope that Aunt Dorrie might come to their rescue died. She began to be afraid that Hilda was going to start crying.

"We have a dog named Fleet," she offered hopefully, watching the younger girl's face with anxious eyes.

Hilda brightened at once.

"Uncle Evan wouldn't let us have a dog," she confided. "Johnny . . . he's Aunt Dorrie's own boy . . . is allergic to their hair. Once Mike found a lost dog and he called her Lady and gave her a bath and everything but Johnny sneezed so much that we had to take her to the Humane Society. What's your dog like?"

"Come on downstairs and I'll show you," Jenny said.

They had shut Fleet in the kitchen just in case his welcome

would be too much for the Jacksons. Hilda went out first.
Jenny glanced back over her shoulder at the room which had
been hers ever since she could remember. Her things were
still there, but, shoved back to make room for Hilda's, they
looked small and lonely.

The boys were clustered in the upstairs hall. Mother, coming to meet them, had just reached the top of the stairs.

"They have a dog, Mike," Hilda greeted her brother.

"Oh," Mike answered. "That's nice," he added hastily, as
her face fell.

"You'll be able to keep this one. Johnny's not here, and they
aren't allergic," Hilda went on.

"Fleet's not his. He's Michael's," Jenny said hotly.

The boy facing her looked confused. He knew that Fleet
was not his, but he was Michael. He wondered suddenly if
Mac's name was really Michael. . . . But if he did not understand, Mother did.

"Don't be silly, Jenny," she said, smiling, but with a sharp-
ness in her voice. "Fleet belongs to all of us. Come on down
for lunch now."

Jenny glared at her mother. Just because this boy was
named Michael and was about Michael's size, was Mother
going to pretend . . .

"I have to get something," she announced, her voice so loud
and sudden that even she knew it was rude. Then, ignoring
the shake of Mother's head, she ran back into her room and
slammed the door.

Mother wanted the boy to take Michael's place! Jenny
pushed away memories of the days before Michael's death,
the days when Mother had told them about the time, before
she was married, when she had worked for the Children's

Aid. Often and often, Mother had told them how hard it was for many foster children who for some reason could not be legally adopted. She had told them about children being shifted from one household to another, never really feeling as though they belonged. She had told them about families being divided. In those days, Jenny had ached inside thinking about them, trying to imagine herself forced to live somewhere with strangers. She had pictured Mother left without Dad, having to let her children go. Whenever she had imagined it, she had felt so frightened that she had crossed her fingers and prayed, "Don't let it really happen. Keep Mother and Daddy safe."

But everything was different now, she defended herself. Her brother was the one who had died. And these Jackson children were not the children she had felt so sorry for. They were real. They were invading her home. And she did not want them.

In one short moment, she would have to go back to them, would have to sit with them and eat and be polite, but for that one moment, she was safe. Her door was shut. All the Macgregors knocked and waited until they were told to come in before they opened a closed door.

Then she heard footsteps. The knob turned. Hilda stood there smiling at her, wriggling a little, like a puppy who sees you are frowning at him, but cannot believe you mean it.

"I waited for you, Jenny," she said. "What did you come back to get?"

Jenny got up off the edge of the bed. It was a hot day but she picked up a sweater that was lying on a chair. There was no reason for Hilda to knock on her own bedroom door. "I'm ready now," she said.

3

At the Quarry

WHEN Jenny and Hilda entered the dining room, Jenny's eyes darted over the waiting table. She and Michael had always sat one on either side of Mother with Alec beside Michael and Mac beside her. Dad did not say much but he knew exactly how to make two small boys behave themselves at the table. After the accident, Mother had moved Mac over to sit beside Alec and Jenny had had one whole side to herself. Today Hilda's chair was next to hers and Michael Jackson was sitting between the younger boys.

Jenny kept her eyes down, examining the spoon and fork in front of her, the napkin opened on her lap, the yellow place mat. She told herself that she was glad the new boy had not been given Michael's place. But, deep inside her, she could feel a seed of disappointment. She had been ready to be furious with Mother again. Now she had no excuse.

"Salt and pepper, please, Jenny," Dad said.

She had to look up. And she had to admit that he just was not like Michael. Michael had had dark hair like hers, a thin brown face, hands that moved wildly while he talked. Michael had loved to talk. Not like Hilda with her steady stream of chatter about everything and anything. He had liked taking hold of one idea — how Indians made canoes, maybe, or why the Leafs were not going to win the play-offs — and explaining it to them excitedly and in great detail, his hands constantly showing them how big or how fast or how wonderful the whole thing was.

This Mike was as tall as their Michael had been, but that was all. He was fair-haired like Hilda. His eyes were blue and they told her nothing. His shoulders were wide where Mike's had been narrow. His hands were wide too, compared to Michael's thin, flashing ones, and they only moved to raise his fork to his mouth or to pass food. Apart from answering questions put to him by Mother and Dad, he said nothing at all.

Then Jenny's attention was drawn to Hilda. She was making a face at the vegetables on the plate in front of her.

"I don't like those," she said, pointing her finger disdainfully at the green beans and carrots. "Aunt Dorrie never makes me eat that stuff."

Glancing across at Mike, Jenny saw his cheeks redden a little, but he went on eating steadily.

"Pass Hilda's plate back," Mother told Jenny.

As Hilda handed her plate to Jenny, she smiled smugly. She thought the whole thing was settled to her satisfaction. Jenny, feeling sorry for her for the first time, knew better.

Mother cut the servings in half and returned the plate. Hilda stared down, horrified, at the small mounds of vegetables.

"But I HATE them!" she wailed. "I can't eat them. They'll make me sick!"

"If you aren't hungry enough to eat, leave whatever you don't want," Mother said. "That doesn't look like too much to me, but you know best whether you're hungry or not. Don't forget there's dessert coming."

The Macgregor children watched Hilda's face brighten. They watched her gobble up her meat and mashed potatoes;

they saw her leave the beans and carrots untasted. Each of of them realized that she did not understand. She did not know Mother. They also knew that even if they had had a chance to warn her, she would not have believed them. She had to find out for herself.

The table was cleared. Mother brought in the chocolate pudding. There was whipped cream to go with it. Hilda beamed.

"I just love chocolate pudding!" she announced.

Jenny, Alec and Mac looked away. Dad coughed and began fiddling with his napkin ring, Mike's chair creaked as he shifted his weight uneasily.

He understands, Jenny thought.

Mother paid no attention to any of them. She smiled straight back at Hilda, gently, sympathetically, very steadily.

"Then it's too bad you weren't hungry enough to finish your first course, isn't it?" she said.

Hilda did not believe it at first. She started to splutter, but under Mother's calm gaze she subsided. Then she just stuck out her bottom lip and tried to will Mother into changing her mind. Mother dished up the pudding. She did not leave even one spoonful in the bowl. Hilda grew very red and started sliding off her chair.

"Just a few minutes more, Hilda," Mother said firmly. "No one leaves the table until we're all finished."

An awkward silence fell while Hilda paused, halfway off her chair, and eyed Mother. Mother smiled around on them all, Hilda included, and said, "This afternoon, if you'd like to go, I thought I'd take you swimming at the quarry."

"Oh boy!" Mac said, forgetting about Hilda.

"As soon as we're done?" Alec asked.

"I don't want to go swimming!" Hilda put in loudly.

Mother turned to her in surprise. "Oh, don't you?" she asked. She looked thoughtful. "Let's see then. While we're away, maybe Mrs. Abbott across the street would . . ."

Hilda had learned a lot in a very short time.

"No, I mean I do want to go," she interrupted hastily, her eyes anxious.

"Fine," Mother said. "We'll leave at two-thirty."

"Lucky things," Dad told them. "It's a hundred-and-five in that library!"

"Poor old Dad," Mac mourned for him, and even Dad laughed.

The Macgregors were taken aback to find that, though both the Jacksons had bathing suits, Hilda could not swim at all and Mike seemed reluctant to enter the deep water. Jenny showed off, cutting through the clear bluish-green water with her best crawl stroke, but when she turned her head, nobody was watching her. Her brothers had found a log and were trying to stand on it. Hilda was crouching in a shallow spot at the edge, looking as though she were afraid to stir. And Mike was on the bank, squatting beside Mother, the two of them deep in talk.

For a moment, Jenny felt cut apart from them all, as though she might just stay far out in the deep water and never go in to where she would have to speak with them or do things with them again. Then she saw Hilda watching her. She swam over to the ledge to which the little girl was clinging like a barnacle.

"Come on," she ordered, her voice loud enough to show the world how little she cared that Mike and Mother were talking to each other. "I'll teach you to swim."

It was not easy. They had to stay on the small rocky ledge where the water was shallow. With Jenny right beside her, Hilda dog-paddled bravely, but Jenny soon saw that she never took both feet off the bottom at the same moment.

"Watch me," Jenny told her over and over again. Hilda watched admiringly. But, even when she saw the water holding every inch of Jenny afloat, she was not convinced that it would do the same for her.

Mike was telling Mother about Aunt Dorrie and Uncle Evan. He was not telling her much. He told her where their house was, what Uncle Evan's job had been, who Aunt Dorrie was, who Johnny was, what Pop did for a living. He did not know that, except when he spoke of his father, there was no warmth in his voice. He was telling Mother more than he guessed. And Mother told him about the other Michael.

"Hilda calls you Mike," she started. "So you like Mike better than Michael?"

Mike nodded.

"I am glad because that way we won't mix your name up with Jenny's twin brother Michael. We never called him Mike. I am not sure why. He was killed in a car accident last December," Mother explained steadily.

Mike did not know what to say. He picked up a small stone with one sharp corner and began scratching squares and triangles in a patch of bare earth at his feet. Squatting there, he could feel the sun getting almost too hot on his back. He heard Jenny urge, "Come on, Hilda. Try! Just try!" He glanced up, avoiding Mother's face, and saw Mac topple off the log for at least the fifteenth time. Water flew in all directions.

"Gee, Mrs. Macgregor," he mumbled, looking down again

and drawing a round face with dots for eyes and a curve for a mouth, "I'm sorry."

He forced himself to look at her and found that she was not watching him at all. She was smiling at the antics of the younger boys. Then she did turn to him, her face warm with kindness.

"I know you are, Mike," she said. She chose her words carefully. "It has been hard for all of us — learning how to go on living without him. Just as you and your father had to learn how to manage without your mother."

Mike tried to bring Mom's face into his mind but it blurred. He went on listening.

"Alec had nightmares for a while after the accident. He was in the car. But he and Mac were always the two younger ones and they made a team just as Jenny and Michael used to. I think that Alec has clung to Mac harder than ever before, though, in the last few months."

Mike dropped his stone and pulled a long stem of grass. He chewed the end of it and made an effort to understand what Mother was trying to tell him. He did not like Alec much. To him, the nine-year-old seemed too sure of himself. He could not really believe that Alec needed anyone to cling to.

"Jenny . . ." Mother's words stumbled and stopped at Jenny's name. Mike was startled. He had never heard her hesitate before, not even when she was speaking of Michael.

"Jenny still worries me." Mother sounded as though she were now talking to herself. Mike had to listen hard to catch the words. "She and Michael looked alike, but in so many ways they were very different. Jenny feels things she can't talk about. She takes life much more seriously than her brother did. I want to help her . . . to keep her from making herself grieve for him when she should be getting on with growing up and learning to laugh. But I can't help her if she doesn't want to be helped. Perhaps she does not grieve for him now. . . . But the way she turned on you about Fleet . . . I just don't know. . . . She and her father are close but they aren't talkers."

Mike waited.

"Mike, I'm sorry," Mother said suddenly, speaking directly to him again. "You should be swimming. I really started to tell you about Michael because I didn't want any more mix-ups like that one this morning and because there are some of his things up in the top shelves of your closet. Those things are yours now and we'll be glad to have them in use again. Michael would be too. He'd be disgusted with me sitting here talking when you should be in that water. Go on and get wet."

Mike eyed the deep water. Neither Aunt Dorrie nor Uncle Evan could swim. The river, for which Riverside was named, was not a good place to learn. It was shallow and rocky, with deep holes in unexpected places, and the water was not clear like this. Mike had nevertheless taught himself an efficient dog paddle. He was not afraid of getting out of his depth. But he was ashamed of his splashing childish stroke when he saw even Mac cutting cleanly through the water, his arms and legs moving together in beautiful rhythm.

"Mother," Jenny yelled suddenly. "Look! Look!"

The two on the bank looked just in time to catch a glimpse of Hilda stretched out in a "dead man's float." The instant they saw her, Hilda realized that Jenny had let go of the straps on her bathing suit. She floundered wildly and sank.

"You did it, Hilda! You did it!" Jenny screamed at her, hauling her up out of the depths. Hilda spluttered, sneezed, coughed, rubbed water out of her eyes and beamed proudly at her teacher.

"Good girl," Mother called.

Jenny looked up eagerly and discovered that Mother was smiling at her, although she had spoken to Hilda.

The two boys, seeing Mike free at last, anchored their ship on a reef near the edge of the quarry and dashed ashore. Mike, who had been soaking up sunlight for the past twenty minutes, dodged their dripping icy hands. There was no escape. He took a deep breath, raced just ahead of them to the edge, and plunged in. As the cold water hit him, he whooped wildly. Then he went under.

Mac and Alec tumbled in after him, whooping just as loudly and churning up the water till Hilda, still on her ledge, clutched at Jenny with panic-stricken hands.

"Boys!" Jenny muttered.

She patted the little girl soothingly.

"It's all right, Hilda. I'll take care of you," she said struggling to keep the impatience out of her words.

"Oh, Jenny, I'm glad you're going to be my sister," Hilda gushed suddenly.

Jenny wanted to swim by herself out in the deep water. She wanted to take the boys' log and lie along the top of it and pretend she was drifting down a great lonely river on her private raft. There was even a part of her that longed to join in the game of water tag the boys were playing now. But she stayed on the ledge with her arm around Hilda's shoulders.

"You floated once," she said, her voice determined. "Let's see you try again."

4

Mike's Private War

ON THE way to the quarry, the three boys had ridden in the back seat. When it was time to go home, the other four children reached the car ahead of Jenny. She hated walking over the sharp stones on bare feet the way the boys did. Hilda, who liked going barefoot no better than Jenny, took only an instant to shove her feet into rubber scuffs, but Jenny had sandals which needed buckling. When she caught up with them, Mac was already settled in the front seat beside Hilda.

Mike saw her pause for an instant before she clambered in beside him. As the car jolted up the gravel road to the highway, she stared intently through the window at the fields and clumps of trees they passed. On the other side of Mike, Alec was studying the countryside with the same determination. Mike saw his rigid pose with surprise. When they were playing in the water, Alec had been gay, confident, even bossy — and Mike saw no reason for his stiff back and stubborn silence now. Up in the front, Mac and Hilda were giggling over "knock-knock" jokes, but Mike never thought to relate Alec's set shoulders to their goofy conversation.

"A rose between two thorns," he thought and grinned to himself.

The Macgregors were certainly prickly right now. Mother's story had made him curious about Jenny. He tried to imagine her twin. Studying her out of the corner of his eye, he struggled to see a boy with her face.

He could not do it. Already her cold green eyes, small straight nose, wide mouth and dark hair — usually curving smoothly by her cheeks but now wind-dried and tangled — made up Jenny and nobody else. She did not like him and he did not blame her. Neither did he care whether she ever changed her mind.

A truck went by with a horse's head poked out through the back and he forgot her.

The next morning he slept late. The Macgregor children, who woke early and completely, were astonished when ten o'clock and then ten-thirty came around and Mike was still not downstairs. At eleven Mother cleared his place off the table and set it again for lunch.

"Wait till you get to be an old man like Mike," she laughed as she caught Mac checking the time and then peering anxiously up the stairs.

"You get up. You're pretty old," he told her.

"Not because I want to." She laughed again. "I think it would be blissful to lie in bed till noon. But the young fry won't let me."

Hilda, who had got up when Jenny did, was embarrassed by the boys' open surprise, by Jenny's scorn.

"That's what people do on weekends," she defended Mike. "Aunt Dorrie and Uncle Evan always sleep in on Saturdays and Sundays."

"Not on Sundays." Alec thought she had forgotten. "You have to get up for church on Sunday."

Hilda wilted under his lofty look, but she stood her ground. "We don't go to church," she told him, trying to sound as uppity as he did.

Jenny smiled. Yesterday, Hilda had been just as sure that she did not eat vegetables. Tomorrow she would find out that in the Macgregor household everybody went to church.

Mike joined them for lunch. He was polite but distant, busy with his own thoughts. Now Jenny was the one who was curious. She watched him, sidelong, just as he had earlier watched her. He was so wrapped up in whatever he was thinking about that he seemed to have forgotten that the rest of them existed.

The saltshaker was sitting right in front of him. Jenny carefully did not look in his direction.

"May I please have the salt," she said into space.

Alec reached across in front of him, picked up the shaker and handed it to her. Mike went on eating steadily. Jenny fumed.

The moment they were excused, Mike disappeared down the street. Jenny had been wishing he would, but she found herself wondering where he had gone. Not feeling in the least like reading, she picked up a book and went out to the hammock. Hilda trailed after her. Mac followed Hilda. Alec, seeing Mac going away from him without a word, snatched up a book of his own, and, seemingly unconcerned, drifted in their wake.

Jenny turned on the lot of them.

"Who said I wanted you kids tagging after me?" she demanded.

"Kid yourself," Alec answered back. He settled himself on the veranda steps, opened his book to pictures of reptiles, and made certain they all realized that he was paying no attention to any of them. He sat so still he might have been waiting for something, but Mac spoke to Hilda.

"Let's swing," he invited.

Hilda stood and looked up at Jenny.

"With her puppy-dog face," Jenny thought.

"Oh, all right. Come on then," Jenny grumbled. She laid her book face-downward in the hammock and gave Alec a meaningful look.

"The hammock's saved."

"Says who?" Alec countered, but he did not look up from his book. Jenny, in the mood for battle, hoped he would try to annex the hammock while she was gone, but she knew he would not. She was a good deal bigger, and Alec never fought unless he was sure of winning. Or, once in a long while, when somebody bigger was foolish enough to try bullying Mac.

"Oh boy!" Hilda grabbed Jenny's hand and dragged her past Alec to the veranda swing. "Are you ever lucky to have a swing and a hammock both! We never had a swing. We used to have to go to the park. There are lots of swings there but mostly you have to wait for a turn."

Hilda filled the swing. She was wider than Jenny, in spite of being so much younger. But Jenny, still feeling a queer warmth which had been born in her heart when Hilda's pudgy fingers closed around hers, pushed her with a will. Hilda squealed happily as the swing swooped higher and higher.

"Jenny, Jenny, she's had long enough. It's my turn." Mac was dancing up and down with impatience.

Jenny grabbed at the rope and stopped the swing. Hilda slid off, landing on the floor with a solid thud. Mac took her place.

"I'll push him," Hilda said eagerly.

"Really high, Hildy," Mac ordered. "Make my toes touch the roof."

Jenny left them. Hilda was at home with Mac. She did not need a big sister to hold her hand. Alec had not moved. Jenny settled herself in the hammock, but not even Mary Poppins having tea standing on her head could hold her attention.

"Where did he go?" she asked Alec offhandedly.

Alec turned the page. "Who?"

Jenny pressed her lips together. He knew perfectly well whom she meant.

"You mean Michael?" he asked, a split second before she would have exploded.

Jenny stiffened at his light use of the name. Her angry eyes met his calm ones. Something in his face made her feel that he had scored a point in some silent war between them.

"Mike," Jenny corrected him, keeping her voice even with an effort.

"I don't know," Alec said.

When Jenny sought shelter behind *Mary Poppins,* he glanced furtively over his shoulder at Mac. Hilda was back in the swing.

"Keep your feet up and I'll give you a run-under," Mac was telling her.

"No, Mac, I'm scared to," Hilda squeaked excitedly.

Alec stared down at a frightening alligator. He did not turn his head again.

Mike was on the other side of town inspecting his tree house. He had built it in the widespread branches of an old apple tree which stood behind a huge tumbledown house three blocks from Aunt Dorrie's. Nobody had lived in the house in all the time Mike had known it and nobody had discovered his tree house last summer or this. You had to slip through a gap in the fence, wade through grass already hip high, push through a tangle of bushes and then, there was his particular secret tree.

But it was not a secret any longer. Mike suspected it when he saw the grass flattened into a sort of path and the bushes bent back and broken so that they would be out of the way. Once he had scrambled up his rope ladder, there was no question. In one corner lay a blanket which he had never seen before, and in the center of the floor, stood a saucer full of cigarette butts and ashes. The licorice whips he had left on the shelf were gone and someone had burned out the batteries in his battered flashlight.

All at once he heard them arriving. He crawled back to the lookout window and stared down into their surprised faces. There were three of them. Mike knew them all; Joey Webster, Nick Zarnoff and Henry Schmitt. They were three or four years older than he and a good deal bigger and broader.

"Hey, kid, what are ya doin' up there?" Joey drawled.

He sounded dangerous, but Mike stayed where he was, his face stubborn.

"It's my place. I built it."

"Whadda you mean . . ." Henry started, glowering up at him. Joey silenced Henry with a swift jab of the elbow.

"Well, gee, kid, thanks a lot," he said smoothly.

Nick shuffled his feet and looked uncomfortable. Mike had always liked Nick. But Joey was the leader.

Henry had caught on and was now leering up at him.

"That was real nice of you, kid, to build us this sweet little joint!" An evil grin split his face.

Joey stopped wasting time abruptly.

"Okay, kid. Out! We've taken over."

"Joey, he DID build it. . . ." Nick ventured.

"Shut up," Joey told him. "Come on, kid. Vamoose."

"I don't have to," Mike said through his teeth. "It's my place. I didn't build it for you. It's mine."

He knew it was useless. Before he had finished, they came swarming up after him. Henry came directly up the ladder. Joey shinned up the trunk, keeping out of range of Mike's boots. Even Nick only hesitated a moment. Mike realized, without having to puzzle it out, that Nick was more afraid of Joey than he was.

As Henry topped the ladder, Mike clouted him with all his strength. Henry shook his head and kept coming. The younger boy tried to beat them off with his fists as they reached for him. He kicked Nick hard on the shin and the boy clutched his leg and yelped with pain. But it was three against one. Nick was up and onto him again in a matter of seconds, and now he was just as angry as the others. After cuffing him a couple of times to teach him manners, they simply bundled Mike out the door and let him drop to the ground eight feet below. Before he could get to his feet, they had hauled up the ladder.

"Scram," Joey yelled down at him.

"And don't bother coming back neither," Henry added.

Mike gathered himself together and left. Every bone in his

body felt jarred, and he knew he would have half a dozen bruises before night. But the worst hurt was the loss of the one place in the world he considered his own.

Throughout the whole long summer and fall before, and from April on this year, he had escaped to the tree house whenever he had had enough of Aunt Dorrie's voice, picking at him, reminding him of all the things he did that he shouldn't and of all the things he didn't do that he should. In her house, he had been an extra child, one too many, a boy underfoot, a mouth to feed, dirt tracked on her polished floors. But in his own house, hidden away in the green branches, he had done no wrong. He had been king.

He took his time returning to the Macgregors'. He went around by the garage where Pop worked, but he was nowhere in sight. Pop had told them not to come to the garage to see him anyway; the boss said they interrupted his work. He had promised to come to visit them on Sunday afternoon.

Mike wandered on, head bent, hands shoved roughly into his pockets. He kicked at a stone, then followed it down the street, kicking it ahead of him each time he caught up with it. It was a long way across town. It had seemed no distance at all on the way over, but now the blocks stretched out endlessly in front of his weary feet. He was half a mile from the Macgregors' house when he noticed that the sun had set and dusk was beginning to fall.

"I won't be there in time for supper," he thought uneasily.

Aunt Dorrie had found fault with him dozens of times for coming in late for meals and he had never let that bother him. But this was different. He had no idea how these people would react.

He was too sore to run but he walked faster. As he neared

his new foster home, he tried to form clear pictures in his mind of the kind of people his foster parents were.

He felt he already knew Mother. (He did not even notice himself calling her "Mother" in his thoughts.) She was the one who did the talking. She was really the boss, he felt.

He remembered hearing Pop say about someone, "She wears the pants in that family."

Mr. Macgregor? He said so little. He was so utterly different from Mike's own father. But when Mike tried to despise him, he felt unsure of himself. The Macgregor children obviously respected their father. They told him things. Even Hilda told him things. And what mystified Mike was the way Dad listened to them. He never said "That's enough now!" sharply, as Pop would have done. When they told him something funny, he laughed as though he enjoyed it as much as they did.

Pop, now, was a talker. He was full of stories and he hated being interrupted. Not that Mike wanted to interrupt. Pop would begin "When I was in the army . . ." or "When I was a boy, we used to . . ." and the two children would listen openmouthed. Long ago, when Mom had been with them, Mike could remember her saying, "Oh, Charlie!" in a scandalized voice when the stories got too colorful. But Pop paid no attention. His boyhood pranks grew more outrageous with every telling. Mike and Hilda gasped when his tiny boat was surrounded by "hundreds of submarines." When Aunt Dorrie complained about Mike, Pop had often brushed that aside too and gone on swapping stories with Uncle Evan.

But what happened at the Macgregors'? Being sent to bed, being told there was no supper left, being lectured for hours, even being spanked . . . Mike had no more time to wonder. He turned down the Macgregor drive.

They had finished supper. Jenny was drying the dishes. Fleet rushed at Mike and jumped up, putting his paws squarely on Mike's chest.

"Hi," Mike said to him.

The loneliness inside him eased a little as Fleet's tongue swabbed across his chin. Mother shook the soapsuds off her hands and took his supper off the stove.

"We saved some for you. Don't worry," she smiled. "You can eat out here. It's homier in the kitchen. Wash your hands in there."

Then she looked at him more closely.

"Well, well," she said, pushing back his hair gently. "What have we here? You must have been in quite a battle."

Mike shuffled, waiting unhappily for the lecture.

"Hurry and get washed before your pork and beans are stone cold," Mother ordered, letting go of him and jerking her thumb toward the washroom.

Mike stared at her. Then he glanced at Jenny. She was standing quite still, her eyes fixed on his battered face. She saw the bewilderment in his eyes, as though Mother had spoken to him in a foreign language. Suddenly she smiled at him, a small, quick ghost of a smile.

Then, as confused as he was, she snatched up the casserole and began to dry it furiously.

5

Can't We Live with You, Pop?

THE next morning, Jenny opened her eyes to see Hilda already out of bed, peering at herself in the mirror. Jenny yawned, said, "Ooooph!" and stretched sleepily.

"I look awful!" Hilda wailed, turning to face her. "Aunt Dorrie would die. She gave me that permanent two weeks ago."

Jenny studied the little girl critically.

The afternoon before, Mother had taken her downtown. When they returned, Hilda had two new dresses, a new hat, a pair of blue jeans, a pair of shorts, shoes that really fit and no curls. The hairdresser had done the best she could to shape what was left, but it was almost as short as Mac's.

"There's a little wave in it," Jenny said comfortingly. "I wish mine waved."

Hilda looked at herself again, more hopefully.

"And don't forget your new dresses," Jenny added.

Hilda smiled.

"I never had a hat before," she confided.

When it came time to leave for church, all five children were lined up in the hall, scrubbed and shining, dressed in their Sunday best. Mike and Hilda looked uncomfortable. Never before had they been so spic and span this early in the morning. And neither of them was quite sure what to expect next. Her new clothes gave Hilda a feeling of excitement, as though she were about to set forth to a birthday party. Mike was resentful.

"My Pop doesn't go to church," he muttered suddenly as Dad stood back inspecting them.

"When your mother and Mrs. Macgregor were little girls, they went to the same Sunday school," Dad said quietly. "And your father is pleased to have you attending church. I asked him. Come on now, it's time we were off."

Sitting in church, Mike noticed the difference in Hilda. She sat up straight and she was quiet and solemn. She had on a round white hat with long ribbons hanging down her back. Her dress was green with a white collar and buttons up the back. The skirt was not too full, the sash was the same green as the dress and there was not one frill. Aunt Dorrie would have a fit if she saw her, Mike thought, and he was pleased.

They sang the children's hymn. Alec and Mac, shepherding Hilda before them, went downstairs to the Primary. Hilda was suddenly overcome with shyness. Her curls, her fancy pink dress had given her courage on the morning she had arrived at Macgregors. But now her dress was plain. Her hair looked like a boy's. And there seemed to her to be hundreds of children all around her, every one of them certain of how to behave and what to do in church.

Alec walked off to his class, but Mac stuck by her. He clutched her elbow with a firm friendly hand. He shoved her toward a tall dark-haired lady with a kind face.

"This is Hilda Jackson, Miss Emerson," he said confidently. "She's never been here before. She's my new sister," he added unexpectedly, his voice proud.

In that moment, Hilda gave her heart to Mac.

Upstairs, the sun was shining through the stained-glass window in the back of the church. Mike began moving his open hymnbook around in the light that was falling into his lap. One moment it was mauve and rose. Then it turned green. Then a deep yellow splashed across it. Color flooded the church making white hats red, and yellow dresses emerald and orange.

Suddenly, Mike looked across in front of Dad and caught Jenny, with the church calendar open in her hands, catching colors just as he had been doing. He grinned. She hastily folded up the calendar and tucked it into the rack which held the hymnals. But Mike saw her lips twitch as though she wanted to laugh. Then, ignoring him completely, she made her mouth prim and looked solemnly at the minister, as though her thoughts had never wandered. Mike wriggled a little, got more comfortable and tried to listen.

That afternoon, Pop came. As he turned up the front walk, Hilda made a face at him from behind the curtains.

"I don't want to stay in here and talk to him," she pouted. "I want to play croquet with Mac."

Mike was shocked.

"Don't say that. You do so want to see him," he hissed at her, afraid that somehow Pop might be able to hear them right through the walls. "He's Pop. He's your father. Your name's not Macgregor. It's Jackson — and don't you forget it!"

But when Pop swung her up into his arms for a hug, Hilda beamed at him.

"See my new dress," she bragged happily. "Jenny says it's 'forest green.' I had my hair cut. Mother made me do it. Wouldn't Aunt Dorrie be mad! Boy, would she ever! I liked my hair curly though, but Jenny says I have a wave, a 'natural wave,' and that is better than a permanent, she says. I have a new hat and new shoes. See. With straps. My toes were pushing against the ends of my old ones."

"Gee whiz, Hildy," Mike groaned. Her words were buzzing around his head like a swarm of bees.

"Hildy?" Pop said, setting her down with a look of relief. "Are you 'Hildy' now?"

"Mac calls me Hildy," she told him. "It's short for Hilda. Everybody in this family has a short name: Jenny, short for Janet; Mac, short for Malcolm; Alec, short for . . . short for . . ."

"Alexander," Mike explained to Pop.

"Hildy, short for Hilda; Mike, short for Michael; even Doug for Douglas — that's Dad — and Liza, short for Elizabeth. That's Mother."

"I don't call them Dad and Mother," Mike put in quickly.

He watched Pop sit down heavily and tried to figure out what could be wrong. Something was. Pop was not himself. He was not hearty and full of talk, as Mike had pictured him only the night before. He was ill at ease. He kept pulling at his shirt cuffs, and already Mike had seen him glance at his watch.

Mike had no way of knowing that it was the difference in Hilda and himself that had robbed Pop of his ready speech. Over the last four years he had grown used to his children and accepted them as they were. Now, seeing them dressed for church and unnaturally well-behaved both because of their clothes and because of his presence, he had suddenly a vision of them as they had been when he last had seen them — a sullen, grubby, untidy boy with a chip on his shoulder and an over-dressed, badly pampered little girl. Hilda was not whining now. Mike was scrubbed, polished, brushed and combed. Their father did not feel he knew them.

"What do you call them?" he asked his son.

"I don't call them anything now," Mike admitted. "I tried calling them Mr. and Mrs. Macgregor, but it sounded queer. Then Mother . . . well, you know who I mean . . . she said I could call them whatever I liked. She asked me what I called you and Mom, and when I told her, she said maybe the easiest way would be to call them Mother and Dad like the others do. But you're my dad!"

"I'm your Pop, Mike," Pop said. "Call him Dad. Call her Mother too. You always called your mother Mom. She's right. It's the easiest on everybody. I don't care."

"You're my father," Mike said stubbornly. Then, for the hundredth time, the question burst out of him. "Can't we live with you, Pop?"

"No." Pop's answer was short.

"Why? Why can't we?"

"You know why not. I've told you often enough in all conscience. I just have one room now. I work nights half the time. When Dorrie was there to watch over you, it was different, but I don't know anybody else like that."

He stopped, looking tired. Hilda took over the conversation again at once, telling him about their trip to the quarry and about her other new clothes. He was very patient with her. Mike felt so lonely he was afraid he might cry. Then Mother brought in tea for Pop, and milk and cookies for the children.

They ate and drank without speaking. Pop got up to go the moment his cup was empty. As he reached the door, Mike

said again, with a touch of defiance in his voice, "You're still my father. Nobody else is my father but you."

Pop halted. Man and boy faced each other across the width of the room. Mike watched his father run his finger around inside his shirt collar as though it felt tight.

"Mike," he said finally, "you have a good home here. I can't take care of you. Why can't you just settle down and try to get along?"

"But, Pop . . ."

"Now, I mean it. I can't take you in with me. I try to explain but you just don't listen. So I'm giving up making excuses and explaining. I want you to do as you're told and stop holding on to me like that. Just . . . settle down and do what you're told."

He hurried off then. They watched him go and waved to him when he looked back. When his old car had pulled away from the curb, Hilda scurried off to find Mac.

Mike, standing alone at the front door and staring down the empty street, was remembering his mother's voice.

"Charlie, I have to have more money for clothes, more money for food. Charlie, why can't you ask for more money? You know you're worth more. You've worked for him for nine years. It's all very well your being such pals but Mike needs a new winter coat. You need a coat yourself. Stand up to him and get your rights, why can't you?"

And he was remembering the way Pop had looked. Angry, bothered, as though he wanted to walk out of the house and not come back. Just exactly the way he had looked at Mike in the few seconds before he drove away.

6

Michael's Watch

THAT night Mike discovered a tennis racquet and a tin of tennis balls in his closet. He examined them hurriedly and then shoved them back out of sight. Mother had said he could have anything he found, but he was sure that to Jenny at least it would look like stealing.

On Monday morning he was up and downstairs in plenty of time to eat breakfast with the family. Jenny pushed her chair back first.

"What are your plans for this morning?" she asked Alec sweetly.

She had heard Mother say that and it sounded natural enough, but when she heard herself saying it, even she was surprised.

Alec stared at her as if he wondered what ailed her. Then he looked at Mac. Finally he said, "I might label my rock collection . . ."

His words trailed off into a half-question, but Mac was not listening. He gulped the last of his milk and gabbled, "Please-excuse-me" at Mother.

"Whoa," Mother said, catching his shirttail as he leaped from his chair. "Wipe off your milky moustache, please. Where are you off to in such a rush?"

"Hildy and I are going to play store," he told her, swiping

at his face with his napkin and leaving half of the ring of milk undisturbed.

Mike waited in his room until he was sure Mac and Hilda would be involved in their game. He did not want his small chatterbox of a sister running after him, demanding where he was going and who had given him the tennis things. When everything seemed quiet, he went into the closet and started taking the racquet out of the press.

Click.

Somebody had turned the knob on his bedroom door. Mike waited, half hidden in the dark closet. The door swung back noiselessly. Alec stood in the opening, looking in.

"What do you want?" Mike growled, stepping out into the room and facing the smaller boy. The tennis racquet lay hidden in the closet.

"I . . . I . . ." Alec stammered, backing away a step.

The hope in his eyes had faded before Mike had seen it was there. His face hardened.

"I'm not hurting you," he said boldly. "I used to sleep in here. I though maybe I'd left some books behind."

Mike knew he was lying, but now Alec seemed very sure of himself. Somehow, Mike felt certain, Alec must know about the tennis racquet. He told himself there was nothing to hide. Mother had told him to use it. But all the years of keeping guilty secrets from Aunt Dorrie had left him with an uneasiness he could not shake. There was no good reason why he had not just walked out with the tennis racquet in his hand when he confronted Alec. But even now Mike was wishing he had shoved it further back into the shadows so that there would be no chance of Alec catching sight of it.

"You stay out of my room," he warned Alec suddenly, advancing upon him. "Stick your nose in here again and you'll be sorry."

The door banged shut. He heard Alec run across the hall and then the slam of another door. Breathing quickly, he ducked into the closet, snatched up the racquet and the tennis balls and left the house. For the first two blocks, he ran. Then, with the Macgregor house and all its inhabitants safely behind him, he slowed to a walk.

He did not come home for lunch. Mother kept his food warm until late afternoon. Then she let Fleet have it. As the family gathered for supper, Mike had still not appeared. Both she and Dad looked troubled.

"Hilda," Dad said slowly, "do you have any idea where Mike has gone?"

Hilda pouted.

"No, I don't. He never tells me anything. He's always going off and just leaving me behind."

"Who'd want to bother taking a little baby girl with them?" Alec asked scornfully.

"Hildy is NOT a little . . ." Mac began.

"Eat your soup, Malcolm," Mother told him.

"Do any of the rest of you know where Mike might be?" Dad persisted.

They shook their heads. Dad looked at Jenny. He went on looking until she blurted:

"How would I know! I've never even spoken to him."

Dad ignored her outburst. He turned to Hilda.

"Alec is right, you know, Hilda," he said quietly. "You aren't a baby but Mike is too grown-up to want to do the things you and Mac like doing. Could he have found somebody his own age in the neighborhood? He must be lonely."

'There isn't anybody his age around here," Mac told his father. "John Marcus and Lefty Nicholson are at camp already and Roger and Susan Hamilton are staying at their grandmother's. Their grandmother wrote and said she'd take the baby and give Mrs. Hamilton a rest but Mrs. Hamilton said the baby was nothing compared to Roger."

Mother and Dad laughed.

"Mac, you should apply for a job on the Riverside *Record,*" Mother said. "You could write the gossip column."

Jenny went on eating her tomato soup. She was Mike's age. That was what Dad meant.

Darkness was falling fast when Mike arrived at the back door. Mother gave him his supper, just as she had done before. He was relieved that she asked no questions, and at the same time he was disappointed. He had found a tennis court and had played for hours. He had bought himself a hamburger with some money Uncle Evan had given him. He had been to a fire, just a grass fire but it was exciting. When he had started home, he had come on a group of children running through a sprinkler, and the cool silver fan of water had been too much for him. He had shed his shirt and shoes and joined them. Afterwards, when he was only a few blocks away, he had taken a wrong turning and found himself wandering in a maze of unfamiliar streets. He had not known before now how frightening it was to walk past house after house, to turn first one corner and then another, and see no person or building that was not strange to you. Then, all at once, he had wound up across the street from the library where Dad worked and he had heaved a sigh of relief.

Mother did not ask and the years of keeping himself to himself were too strong in him.

"Upstairs now and get out of those clothes," Mother said crisply, as he took his last bite of johnnycake. "I have a feeling those jeans are damp."

Mike was astonished. He looked down at himself, but he could see nothing that would have told Mother he had been dripping wet three hours before. (The Macgregors could have told him that their mother had a sixth sense when it came to damp clothing or the beginnings of a cold or a lie being told.)

"Thanks for the food," he said awkwardly.

"That's what I'm here for." Mother grinned at him. "Now get."

He was shedding his clothes when he heard a knock on his door for the second time that day. There was no mistaking this one. Mike's heart plunged into the neighborhood of his stomach. He had known all along, he had been positive that somebody would do something.

"Come in." He tried not to quaver the words.

As he had expected, Dad opened the door. But the interview was not what Mike had expected at all. When it was over, Mike thought back over it trying to make sense out of it.

First Dad had handed him a watch. It was a good watch. He had never had a watch before and this one looked fine on his wrist. It had been Michael Macgregor's.

"Now you won't have any trouble getting home in time to eat," Dad had said dryly. His voice had sounded stiff to the listening boy. "We expect you to let Mrs. Macgregor or myself know, from now on, if you are going to go out of earshot of the house," he had continued.

If he caught sight of Mike's horrified expression, he did not acknowledge it directly. But he added, "You don't have to account for every minute of your time. But we have to have

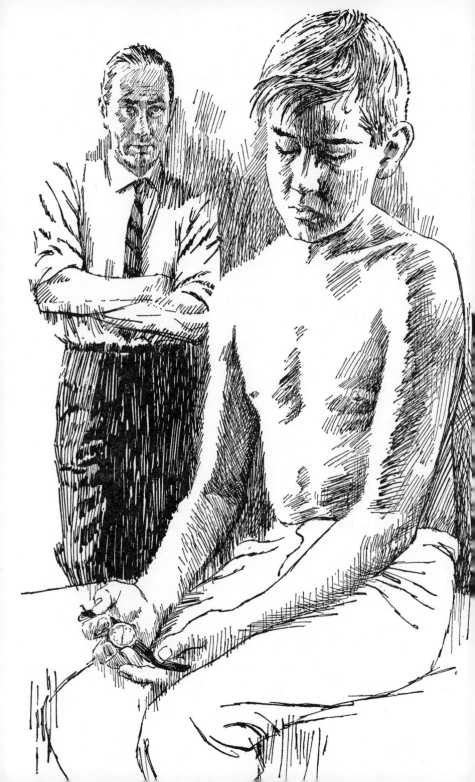

some idea of the direction you are heading in, and about when you plan to return. If you can't get home, phone and explain."

He paused, fished in his pocket and pulled out fifty cents.

"Here is your allowance. The others got theirs at noon. If you plan to miss many meals, you'd better save your money for telephone calls. . . . Your father called you today."

Mike's eyes had jerked up from the coins in his hand to search Dad's face.

"Pop . . . called ME?"

"Yes. He phoned at lunchtime when he was sure you would be home. He phoned again before supper. He seemed worried about you. I had to tell him that you had not come home and that we had no idea of where you might be. I called his boardinghouse just before I came up and left word that you were back safely."

Mike had not known what to say. The whole world seemed to be switching sides on him. This man who had just given him a watch and money of his own still seemed so curt and faraway that Mike, who hardly understood his feelings himself, could not possibly have put them into words for Dad.

"He's shy and he's thinking that he isn't really your father," Jenny would have told him, but Jenny had not spoken to him yet and Jenny was not there to help him now.

He had thought, in a bewildered fashion, of Aunt Dorrie. She had never cared where he went as long as he kept out of her way. She had nagged, but she had never really cared. And Pop! Pop "seemed worried" about him. But Pop had never asked questions before either. And just yesterday, he had told Mike to leave him alone! Or, at least, that was what Mike had understood him to be saying.

No one had ever made it a rule that Mike had to explain where he went and what he did if he were going off the block. No one had ever insisted on being told when he planned to come home.

Then, from somewhere deep in his heart, he heard Mom saying to a much younger Mike, whom he could hardly recognize as himself, "You can go out and play, Mike, but don't go out of sight or sound of the house. When I call you, I want you in here lickety-split."

"Sleep well, Mike."

Dad's voice broke right into the middle of Mike's confused thoughts. Then, without asking for any promises, without lecturing, without waiting to be thanked for the watch, Dad was gone.

It was a long time before Mike slept at all.

7

Fresh Starts

ON THE way downstairs Jenny promised herself, for the hundredth time that morning, that she would speak to Mike. She had tried to plan speeches but nothing sounded right. Friday, Saturday, Sunday and Monday had passed without her addressing him directly, and now it seemed an impossible task.

He was already at the table when she came in. She gulped, opened her mouth and said, "Good morning." She could not quite manage "Mike."

"Good morning," he answered. His tone was guarded but not unfriendly.

"Oh, wonderful!" Jenny sang inside herself as she slid into her place. "Oh, I did it and it was so easy."

She looked, half shyly, at Dad and caught his smile of congratulations.

Then Alec spotted the watch on Mike's wrist. For a second he was not sure, but then, as Mike reached for the milk, he saw clearly the familiar squarish face and the dark leather strap.

"You have my brother's old watch," he said.

It was a statement, not a question. Alec enjoyed surprising people with bits of information which he picked up by keeping his eyes and ears open and on the alert. For once, Mike did not hear the smugness in the younger boy's voice. He saw

Jenny's eyes fly to his wrist, the brightness drain from her face, her hand stop in midair on its way to the honey. Then her lids dropped quickly, hiding whatever she felt. She pulled the honey pot toward her.

"I gave it to him," Dad said calmly.

He finished off his coffee hurriedly, excused himself and left the room. Jenny spread honey on her toast, slowly, evenly. Mike wished she would look up. Then, shrugging, he swallowed his last bite of toast and pushed back his chair.

He was halfway to his feet before he remembered. He flushed. "Excuse me," he mumbled.

"Certainly." Mother did not seem to see his reddened cheeks. Then, as he really stood up, she went on talking to him.

"You know, Mike," she said, pausing to take a slow sip of coffee, "when I was about your age I went to live with my Aunt Marie for six months."

Mike saw the Macgregor children's faces grow expectant. Mac even stopped eating to listen.

"Well, Aunt Marie lived in an old, old house and she had a maid. The maid even wore a little frilled cap and an apron. And when Aunt Marie wanted her to serve the table, she pressed a button under the carpet with her foot and a bell rang in the kitchen. The maid was almost as old as she was and my parents had taught me always to stand up when an older person came into the room. So on my first night there, when Geraldine came in to the dining room, I naturally stood up. Not only that, I started to gather up dishes to help carry them to the kitchen. In my home everyone helped. I can still remember the scandalized look on Aunt Marie's face and the equally scandalized look on Geraldine's. Aunt Marie hissed,

'E-liz-a-beth!' at me, as though I were some kind of wild animal, and Geraldine said, 'No, no, Miss. Don't get up, Miss.' "

"What did you do?" Hilda asked, sympathy on her round face.

"I sat down in a hurry," Mother confessed. "But that wasn't all. When the dessert came, it was a little square of plain cake and a dish of fruit. I began on the fruit . . . preserved peaches, I think it was . . . and then I reached out, picked up my cake and took a big bite out of it. Wouldn't you have done the same?" she appealed to them.

"What else could you do?" Hilda wanted to know, while Jenny, Alec and Mac all nodded vigorously.

Mother laughed. "It seems funny now, although I felt absolutely awful then," she admitted. "Aunt Marie just gave me another look, coated with ice inches thick, and asked, 'Is that cake fork too small for you to see it, Elizabeth?' We used forks for cake at our house only if it was too gooey to hold in our hands. We were always saving dishes since we had to do them ourselves. But of course, Aunt Marie never dreamed of doing dishes. Poor old Geraldine did them all alone. Even when I dared to offer to help, days later and behind Aunt Marie's back, she wouldn't let me get anywhere near them. They had a complete set of dishes, twelve of everything, for just the two of them, and Geraldine had been washing and drying them for nearly forty years and had not broken one yet. Aunt Marie had a husband but he was always away. I used to think he must be as uncomfortable there as I was."

Mike laughed with the others and escaped. This time he understood what Mother was telling him. Mother, too, had found it hard to learn different customs. She had experienced the same embarrassment he felt often these days for both himself and his sister. And Mother did not think they were badly brought up children, as he had been sure she must. She knew that things were done differently in different homes. Suddenly he could just see her putting her foot into it at her aunt's. Just one girl left alone in a house with two old sticks like that — for six months. If he had to spend the rest of his life at the Macgregors', he thought, it couldn't be as bad as that.

He paused on the back steps. The whole long sunny morning stretched invitingly before him. Fleet crowded close to him on the step and Mike's heart warmed with love.

"What do you want, you old hound?" he asked the dog.

But he knew what Fleet wanted. Nobody had openly put it into words yet, but Fleet had adopted this boy. Since Michael's death, Fleet had slept in the kitchen, but on Sunday night when Mike's light was out and he was almost asleep, his bedroom door had been nudged open. Toenails had clicked across the tile floor toward him. A wet cold nose had sniffed up and down the length of the bed as though making sure the right person was in residence. Then, with a contented sigh, Fleet had curled himself up on the hooked rug, and after a few thumps and snorts had settled himself for the night. He had been there again last night. And this morning, it was clear, he had decided that the time had come to look after this boy in daylight too.

But where were they going to go? Mike's jaw hardened. He would not go back in there, as though he were no bigger than Mac, and tell Mother he and Fleet were off in search of adventure but would be back for dinner.

"Come on, boy," he yelled suddenly to the dog.

Fleet galloped after him, his tail flying like a banner. Side by side, they tore the length of the yard. The dog braced his forefeet and skidded to a halt before he reached the fence, but the boy let himself thud against it with abandon. Then, some of his excess energy gone, he started to explore. He knew what he was looking for, and at last the two of them found it.

Right on the Macgregor property, definitely within earshot of the house, was a place where, if he worked carefully, he would be able to build himself a wonderful secret hideout without anyone suspecting.

"Don't give me away, Fleet," he whispered.

The setter seemed to walk more quietly in answer.

Mike began work at once. It was not easy but he enjoyed himself more than he had in months. The day was gone before he knew it. He was right on time for every meal.

"Where were you, Mike?" Hilda quizzed him.

"Oh, around," he said vaguely.

"Where?" she persisted.

"Eat your supper, Hilda, and leave your brother in peace," Mother said. She took the sting out of the words with a special smile.

They went to the quarry again Wednesday. This time, Dad came too. He watched the boys splashing about for a few minutes and then he called, "Mike."

Mike came, wondering what could be wrong. Jenny, catching the uneasiness in his face, was astounded. Dad was so easy to get along with, so much a part of herself. She had not needed words from him to know how he felt after Michael's death. He had always read to the older two while Mother read to the little ones. After the funeral was over and the family was beginning to try ordinary living again, he had brought home Rosemary Sutcliff's books from the library.

One after another, he had read them aloud to her. And as Jenny shared the heartbreak and loneliness of Beric, Tamsyn, Drem and the rest, her own heartache was eased and she began to share in the beauty and the hope in the stories — the colors of flowers she had never seen, the spring weather, the love of animals, the inner light of kindness. Remembering all this, she missed what Dad said to Mike, but a few seconds later she saw them working together until Mike could do the crawl better than Mac and almost as well as she did it herself.

Plowing through the water, his feet churning steadily behind him, Mike felt a new kind of power. Although Dad said nothing more personal than, "Keep your knees straight . . . turn your head . . . Fine, that's it . . ." Mike felt almost at ease with him for the first time.

They had a picnic supper. Haltingly, he and Jenny began to talk to each other as they ate. They were in the same grade at school. He liked science and history. She hated history but she enjoyed science too. Her favorites were arithmetic and literature. They sat side by side, toasting marshmallows on long pointed sticks. And a truce grew up between them. They were far from being friends, but she let him know that he was no longer her enemy and he began to relax with her. Both of them forgot he was wearing Michael's watch.

That night, when they reached home, Mac begged that they sing for a while before he and Hilda had to go to bed. Mother looked at the time and started to shake her head, but Dad came in on their side and led her to her place at the piano.

"I want 'Found a Peanut,'" Mac announced.

"Nothing doing," Mother told him. "I am going to choose

the songs — one for each of you — and then, bed and no back talk."

Mike stood back, watching, not one of the group. Then he saw that Hilda also felt left out and he moved closer and put his hand on her shoulder.

"Hilda's a wonderful singer," he said loudly. "She sang a solo in her class's Christmas concert last year."

The Macgregors beamed at Hilda, and Mike felt her straighten and stick out her chin.

"We'll sing one for Hilda first, one we all know," Mother said.

She swept into "Home on the Range," and next thing Mike knew, everybody was singing lustily, himself included. Mother played "Clementine" for Mac, "Waltzing Matilda" for Alec, "A Capital Ship" for him. Then the notes grew softer till they sounded like lullaby music.

"What shall we sing for Jenny-short-for-Janet?" Mother asked. " 'Working on the Railroad' is not the best song to put you two in a sleepy frame of mind."

"My solo was pretty," Hilda said bashfully. "It started 'The shepherds had an angel.' "

"We know that one," Mac told her.

At the same moment, Alec scoffed, "That's a Christmas song, stupid. It's summer now."

"It's lovely, Christmas and summer both," Mother silenced him. "Just a moment. Here it is. Number 601 in the hymnal."

She began to play very softly. Hilda's voice rose as sweet and clear as a small bird's, but Jenny's had a catch in it, as though she were thinking of the little lost lambs.

They sang all the verses through, but it was the first two

that were to go on singing themselves in Jenny's and Michael's minds in the days ahead.

> *The shepherds had an angel,*
> *The Wise Men had a star,*
> *But what have I, a little child,*
> *To guide me home from far,*
> *Where glad stars sing together,*
> *And singing angels are!*

> *Lord Jesus is my guardian,*
> *So I can nothing lack!*
> *The lambs lie in his bosom*
> *Along life's dangerous track;*
> *The willful lambs that go astray*
> *He, bleeding, fetches back.*

Mother got up very quietly and stretched out a hand each to Mac and to Hilda.

A few minutes later, going along the upstairs hall, Mike heard Hilda singing to herself in the tub . . .

> *The Wise Men had a star,*
> *But what have I, a little child,*
> *To guide me home from far . . .*

He slammed into his room, shutting out her voice, but not quite shutting out his feeling that the two of them had been at "home" all day. He was going to live with Pop, though! Someday he and Hilda were going to have a real home.

The queer tune kept on singing inside his head, but he

wrenched his thoughts away from it. He had his secret place to think about. He had plans to make.

"Tomorrow's going to be a busy day, Fleet," he said, "a very busy day!"

8

Jenny Has to Know

ON THURSDAY, he discovered the junk heap behind one of the factories down by the river.

"I . . . I'm just going to look around the neighborhood," he had explained awkwardly to Mother, waiting until the others had gone before approaching her. "I'll watch the time though and I'll be home for lunch."

Mother had gone on stacking dishes calmly.

"That's fine, Mike. Have a good morning," she said over her shoulder.

He liked her, he thought, as he investigated the treasure trove he had found. Here was wood enough. Here were nails too. He knew the drawer where the hammer was kept. He could borrow it and have it back again without anyone knowing. Sorting through the rubbish, he went on thinking of Mother. The way she had just let him go! No "Is your room tidy?" Not even "Well, see that you ARE back by lunchtime!" Just "Have a good morning."

It was a whole week before Jenny managed to uncover his secret. They were not friends. She had never yet called him Mike in the casual way the others did. She still thought out her words before she spoke to him. But there was nobody else to do things with, and the summer days were so long. She read. She practiced on the piano. She even played house with Mac and Hilda once. She helped her mother in the kitchen. And all the time, she wondered where Mike went and what he did. He was home for meals, but although she watched, she could never figure out where he came from. It seemed that each time Mother had just asked her to pour the milk, or she had turned to order Alec to leave her book alone before he lost her place, or Dad had come in and she had gone to kiss him hello — and there was Michael. It was as though someone waved a wand and made him appear out of thin air.

Once she had the bright idea that if she could catch Fleet apart from Michael, the dog might lead her to the boy. But Fleet was never to be found apart from Mike. His desertion hurt Jenny, but even she could see that Mike took proper care of the setter, brushing him regularly and exercising him every day. She had to admit to herself that her brother would have been delighted to see Fleet's shining coat.

Every morning when the dog and boy set out from the house, she hurried as fast as she could without drawing attention to herself to a window. But Mike was careful to take a roundabout route to his hideout.

"One of these days, I'll just plain follow him," Jenny muttered — but so far, she lacked the courage.

On Wednesday afternoon, when Mike and Hilda had been living with them for almost two weeks, Jenny came home from the library and went upstairs to put her books in her room. As she passed Mike's door, she listened. She was certain he was not there. He had gone again . . . wherever it was he went.

"Not that I care," she told herself, going in and dumping the books down on her dresser with unnecessary violence. It was terribly hot and she was terribly bored. She wandered to her window and stood looking out over the flat roof of the Markhams' house into the street beyond. It was empty. As Mac had said, every child in the neighborhood, every child anywhere near her age, was out of town.

All at once, she stopped staring at the deserted street below and went swiftly across the hall to Michael's room. For an instant, she stood and listened, once again, to the stillness inside. Then she reached out and gave the door a gentle tap with the tips of her fingers. It opened a little.

"I know where he is," Alec said behind her.

Jenny whirled on him, choking back a scream. Her hands shook. Her eyes blazed.

"You . . . you sneak!"

Alec just looked at the door which she had pushed open so quietly. Fairly caught, Jenny was speechless for a long moment. Alec did not mention the door.

"I know where he is," he said again. He was boasting, but he spoke very quietly. "I can show you what he has been doing, if you want."

Jenny opened her mouth to refuse hotly, but he said, "He's away now. He won't know you saw."

Jenny hesitated, but she had to know.

"Okay," she said, her voice low, her eyes not meeting his.

"You give me a dime and I'll show you," Alec said calmly.

"I haven't got a dime."

Alec's eyes narrowed.

"You have so. I saw it in your drawer. With your hair clips. You'll have to hurry," he pressed her, as she stood uncertainly.

"You stay out of my dresser," she ordered. She was angry, but still she wanted to know what he had discovered. "I'll tell Mother on you if you snoop into my things."

They both knew it was an empty threat. She went for the dime. As she got it out of the drawer, she felt like somebody else, someone ashamed and even afraid, and yet excited in a queer, dangerous way. She remembered a movie she had watched on T.V. one afternoon when she had had to stay home with a sore throat. There had been a blackmailer in it who had arranged to meet the heroine in a dark alley. He had been quiet and deadly and somehow . . . just like Alec. But Alec was only her little brother!

She joined him and handed over the money silently. He pocketed it just as silently, and then led her down the stairs, along the hall, through the living room, out the side door, across the veranda and into the yard.

They both moved like spies. Watching Alec as he slid along in front of her, Jenny understood how he had come up behind her without her knowing. He had always been quiet. They even called him "The Thinker" and kidded him about never saying much. Had he always been quiet in this eerie way? Jenny did not think so, but she was too preoccupied to wonder about it now.

"Sh," he said. He paused, looking around. Then he moved forward, eased open the small door into the back of the garage and disappeared into the shadows inside.

Jenny halted.

"Come on."

In spite of herself, she obeyed the whispered command. She stood beside him, waiting for her eyes to grow accustomed to the darkness.

"See." His voice was thin as a thread.

She peered around. In winter, Dad cleaned out the garage and parked his car there, but in summer, he gave up and left it in the driveway. Jenny saw the usual clutter — garbage cans, a lawn chair missing one leg, the ladder, piles of old newspapers, a rake and the lawnmower, the croquet set. . . .

"Look up, you dope," Alec said. "There."

Jenny saw it. Right above her head, under the slanted tin roof, a hut had been built across the rafters.

"Oh!" she cried, right out loud.

Alec shushed her immediately.

"How does he get up there?"

Her brother gave her a look of pure scorn. He pointed. Against the far wall dangled a short rope ladder.

"I told you I knew where he went," Alec bragged. Then, as noiseless as ever, he was back at the door. "We'd better leave before he gets back. 'Bye."

She took one step after him. Then she paused. She could not leave yet, not for a minute or two anyway. She wound her way forward through the collection of odds and ends until she stood directly beneath the rope ladder. It hung from a pitch-black hole, big enough for a boy Mike's size to crawl through. The bottom of the ladder dangled about two feet over her head.

It looked so dark up there. Anyway, how could she ever climb that ladder!

Ten minutes later, Jenny was crossing the veranda again. This time, she was alone. In the pocket of her blue jeans were three matches and a candle end.

She had to know, she just had to know what was up there!

9

Please, Jenny, Jump!

JENNY had to put a box on top of Mac's wagon before she was up high enough to climb the rope ladder. She knew that her brother Michael would have swung himself up easily with only his hands, but she never had been a daring climber. Whenever they had climbed a tree, he had been at the top in a minute, seeming to her to fly up like a monkey, while she had struggled to get herself astride the bottom branch. This Mike was probably just as agile.

Once she had wriggled through the door hole, she crouched in semi-darkness and fished out her stump of candle. That candle had been standing on a saucer on top of the upstairs hall bookcase ever since the electricity failed during a thunderstorm almost three weeks ago. She felt very smart to have thought of it.

The first match broke as she tried to strike it. The second flared up into sudden flame and she dropped it hastily, afraid of burning her fingers. It glowed momentarily and then went out. As she struck the third and last one, she held her bottom lip between her teeth. "Please, light properly," she said, under her breath, "Please." The flame flickered wildly. Then it steadied, and with a sigh of relief, Jenny got the candle lit.

From the instant she first looked around, she loved Mike's hideout. It had three walls, one being formed by the garage wall and the other two pieced together out of odd-shaped lengths of boards and some joining pieces of cardboard. The fourth side had been left open, partly to let in a little of the dim light inside the garage and partly as a lookout post. On one of the walls, Mike had tacked up a shelf. Over it, a light bulb dangled on the end of a cord which had been threaded in through a hole by one of the rafters. Examining it, Jenny realized that he must have had to crawl out along the narrow beam to install the extension cord which joined his light onto the garage light. She shuddered at the thought.

She reached out to turn on the electricity but drew back her hand. She felt safer in the soft glow which fell from her candle. If she heard him coming, it would take just a puff to put it out. She started to wiggle closer to see what he had on his shelf. Hot wax dripped on her hand.

"Ouch," she whispered.

Carefully, she tilted the bit of candle and held it until a pool of wax had formed on the floor. Then, quickly, she stood the candle upright in the pool and pressed it down firmly. When she let go, it stayed in place, burning steadily. She wondered if Mike would notice the little spot of wax in the corner, sometime after she had gone. Even if he did, he would never know how it came there.

Mike came home by the back way. He was lugging the basket part of a wicker chair. How he was going to get it up into his hut he had no idea, but he was delighted to have captured it. He cut down the next-door driveway and lowered the chair over the Macgregors' fence into the little space between the fence and the garage.

Then he boosted Fleet over after it. Fleet was getting expert at giving a spring with back legs, catching the top of the fence with his front paws and scrambling over. Mike always gave a helpful shove at just the right moment. He climbed over himself.

Now, leaving the chair where it was, he strolled casually into the yard and looked around. Nobody was in sight. Mike did not see Alec flattened against the maple tree. The lawn sprinkler was going. Dad must be home. "Okay, boy," Mike said. They went back for the chair. As he lugged it into the garage, Mike banged against a garbage can Jenny had shifted earlier.

In the hut above him, Jenny spun about to put out her candle. As she whirled, her foot knocked against it. It toppled over against the hideout wall. Jenny reached for it, but it was too late. Even as she put out her hand, a long strip of cardboard caught fire. A thin flame licked up the edge of the wall.

Mike saw it only a second after Jenny did. He saw Jenny, too, through his lookout window. Her eyes were wide with horror. He saw her hands pushing at the air in front of her as though she were somehow keeping the fire from reaching her.

He dropped the basket chair and ran for the rope ladder.

"Here, Jenny!" he shouted up at her. "Come down here. Come down the ladder!"

But she couldn't. The way to the ladder was already blocked. The flames crackled out across the opening fiercely. Mike tore back to the center of the garage, thrusting past whatever got in his way. Jenny was cowering back against the other wall now, staring at the yellow flames. He saw her cringe away from the hot breath of the fire. She looked queer in the dancing light, queer and unreal and terribly afraid.

"Jenny!" Mike yelled frantically. "There's no wall on this side! Jump, Jenny! Jump!!"

His voice reached her. She edged over to the open side. She looked down at him through the lookout space. Then she just crouched there.

"Please, please, Jenny," Mike begged. His voice was hoarse with terror. "Please jump!"

Then Dad was there. He looked up at Jenny.

"Jump," he said.

Jenny saw him with eyes that did not seem to know who he was. Mike was crying now, crying and shaking all over.

Dad held up his arms to her.

"Jump, Jenny," he said.

For one nightmare moment, Mike thought she was going to stay there, looking down at them, her face twisted and sick. Right in front of him, she was going to burn to death.

"Jump right now," Dad ordered mercilessly.

Jenny shut her eyes. Through the snapping of the fire, Mike heard her sob once. Then she jumped into her father's arms.

10

Jenny Alone

DAD was knocked back a step, but he kept his balance and he kept a tight hold of the tangle of arms and legs that was his daughter. He held her so close that she felt his heart hammering against her, and when he let out his breath, it was as though she herself had given a great sigh. Then, without a word to her, he pulled free her clutching hands and set her on her feet abruptly.

"Mike," he barked, "get that hose in here!"

Jenny's legs wobbled under her like the flimsy legs of a pipe-cleaner doll. She half-sat, half-leaned on a garbage can and shook her head suddenly and violently, trying to put herself back in the real world. She heard Fleet, ordered to stay outside, whimpering with fright. She saw Mike race through the garage door and disappear. She saw, not stopping to wonder how or why, that Alec was here too, standing just behind Dad. His hands were balled up into fists. His face blazed with excitement. She saw, although she tried to keep from seeing, the fire above them. Most of the hut was burning now. One of the rafters had caught. Sparks were starting to shower down on the jumble of things below.

Dad took her by the shoulder, grabbed Alec by one arm and pushed them out into the yard. Mike, drenched to the skin, was dashing toward them carrying the hose with the sprinkler still attached and flinging its wide circle of water.

Dazed as she was, Jenny instinctively ducked as Mike passed, but an icy stream of water swept her shoulder and slapped against her left cheek with unexpected force. She gasped, rubbed the water out of her eyes, and came awake for an instant.

"Don't go in there," she moaned, but whether she was talking to Mike, who was disappearing into the garage, or to her father, whom she could see waiting just inside the door, she did not know herself.

Dad took time to unscrew the sprinkler. He had the hose free in a matter of seconds, but to each of the watching children he seemed to be wrestling with it for a long time.

"Stand back," he barked at Mike. Mike jumped to safety just as a sheet of cardboard came loose and fell flaming at his feet. Jenny was beginning to slip back into a dream world again. She saw Mike jump on the cardboard and trample out the flames. Her father had disappeared, but she could hear a stream of water drumming against the rafters. At first, there was the sound of the jet of water and the snap of the fire together. Then, little by little, the hammering of the water drowned out the noise of flames. Another piece of cardboard came hurtling down, but this time Mike did not need to stamp on it. It was already soggy.

"It's still sizzling," Alec said once.

Jenny did not answer. She was watching the wall of the garage just inside the door. The strange light which had flickered back and forth there at first, was there no longer. The sound of the water went on, back and forth, back and forth.

"That's done it," Dad said at last.

He climbed down from his perch on a broken lawn chair

and looked around for the sprinkler. It had rolled into a corner. Mike fetched it, but he did not look up at Dad's face when he handed it to him. Dad looked at the sprinkler and then at the water which spurted from the hose.

"Go and turn off the tap, boy," he ordered.

Head down, not looking at either Jenny or Alec, Mike dog-trotted across the yard and turned off the outside spigot. His blue suit soaked, his shoulders and head gray with ash, Dad came out into the sunlight. He screwed the sprinkler back in place. When he had put the hose back in a position to water the rose bush and the corner flower bed and had had a moment to back out of range, Mike turned the tap on again.

Now, at long last, Dad turned and looked at Jenny. He was standing close to her. The sharp smell of wet smoke stung her nostrils. He looked very big, bigger than she had ever seen him before. Then, all in one instant, Jenny's pipe-cleaner legs caved in under her. She felt herself folding up, the world tipped sideways and everything swam in a bright blur before her. Dad caught her as she started to fall.

"Come with me," he said, over his shoulder, to the two boys.

Jenny closed her eyes and let her cheeks rest on his damp lapel. She felt as though she had climbed mountains and fought wars and faced dragons all in the last hour. When they reached the back door Mike sprang ahead of them and opened it.

"Thank you, Michael," Dad said.

"Jenny!" Mother's voice sounded queer. "Doug . . . What is it? . . ."

Jenny's eyelids flew up. She raised her head and looked at Mother.

"What on earth have you been doing?" Mother said.

Jenny decided she had imagined the funny faraway note in Mother's voice. Mother was her usual matter-of-fact self. She had turned to Mike, who was shivering in the open doorway.

"Whatever happened, you are getting into a hot tub in about two seconds flat, Mike Jackson," she told him.

"Between them, they set the garage on fire. If Alec hadn't had sense enough to come running for me, they'd be cinders by now, I imagine," Dad said. "Now go and get clean. You can put on your pajamas and stay in your rooms till I come. There you are, Janet. That is as far as this free ride goes."

Again, he set Jenny on her feet; again, he was not too gentle about it.

Mother went ahead with Mike. Jenny trailed along. By the time she reached the top of the stairs, she could hear Mike's bath running.

"Hurry up, Jenny," Mother said, whisking past her down the hall.

Jenny undressed slowly. Her hands were unsteady. When she was ready for the tub, she pulled her dressing gown around her and sat on the edge of Hilda's bed, staring down at her bare toes. They burrowed deep into the rug Mother had hooked for her long ago. It had a picture of a gray kitten on it. Jenny planted one foot squarely on the kitten's demure face.

"Your turn," Mother said. She scooped up Jenny's dirty clothes and led the way to the bathroom. She said nothing about the fire. She scrubbed Jenny thoroughly as though she were still a baby who could not wash herself. Then she hustled her into her pajamas and ushered her back into the bedroom.

"Thank goodness for Alec," Mother said — and disappeared.

Jenny stretched out on her bed and lay very still, looking at the ceiling. Because of her, the nicest hideaway place she had ever seen had been ruined. Because of her, Mike was in serious trouble. Trouble for both of them had been obvious in the set of Dad's jaw when she had come upstairs.

And Alec must have been spying, or he would never have known anything had gone wrong in the garage. He had saved her life by running for Dad, but she did not care. He was still a tattletale and a little sneak.

She turned over on her stomach and buried her head in her arms. Not that she was going to cry! She never cried. But she had spoiled Mike's hideout . . . and she did not know how to talk to Mother any more.

Even to herself, Jenny could not explain what exactly she felt had gone wrong between Mother and her. Until Michael had been killed, Mother had been just the way mothers are supposed to be. She had called them to meals and read stories to them and laughed at their jokes and lost her temper at them and kissed them good-night. Jenny still shrank from remembering those first days without Michael. Every time they sat down to eat, he was not in his place. When she passed his bedroom door, she would see into his room — everything put away, no books open on the desk, no wrinkles in the bedspread, no sound at all. Dad had closed the door, but that had made it worse. Then Mother had shifted all the furniture around and had moved Alec in there.

Perhaps that night had been the night when it had started — this strangeness between them. Jenny had been in her own room, sorting through a big box of ancient paper dolls she had found, when she had heard a thud and then a scraping noise from across the hall. She had sat perfectly still, listening. Someone had walked across Michael's floor. Jenny had put down the paper doll twins and gone to the door.

Across the hall, Michael's door stood open. Mother was standing on a step stool, hanging yellow and tan striped curtains. She glanced over her shoulder and caught sight of Jenny watching.

"Come and hand that curtain up to me, dear, will you please?" she had said.

She had not mentioned Michael. For the first time, Jenny had felt shy about speaking of him. When they had finished putting up the curtains, the two of them had made the bed with fresh sheets. Then Mother had sent her to get Alec's clothes from the dresser and closet he shared with Mac.

She had almost said, "I miss Michael so much," when she came back; but Mother had seemed so busy, and of course, Jenny had told herself, Mother must be missing Michael too . . . probably a lot more than she did. Without a word, Jenny had gone ahead and arranged Alec's underwear in neat piles, far neater than those in her own dresser.

Now she came back to the present with a jolt. She turned over onto her back again, jouncing so hard that the bed squeaked. Mother was still Mother. She still cooked and sewed and scolded and laughed. It must be that she, Jenny, was making the whole thing up.

But there had been other times. There had been the day Jenny had been sitting holding the butterfly collection she and Mike had started two years ago. There were only five butterflies in the box and two of them were the same kind. Jenny was hugging the box against her, remembering the fun they had had catching those five, although she couldn't watch when Michael killed them. "And now," she had thought, "Michael is dead. Why?" But when Mother found her, she had sent her to the store for a dozen eggs. When she came back, the box was gone.

And Michael's clothes and his schoolbooks had all disappeared in the same way. She was sure Mother had done it, although she had not seen her.

Usually when Jenny was sent to her room, she felt it was cheating to read. You forgot all about whatever you had done wrong two minutes after you opened a book. But now she jumped off the bed and went to the bookcase. She wanted a book. She wanted a sad book. She was not ashamed of crying over people in a story. She chose *The Birds' Christmas Carol* and curled up in the chair next to the window. Soon she was in another world, where Mother, the two Michaels, and the nightmare of fear she had felt when she had been trapped by the fire could not follow her.

11

Dad's Verdict

IN THE garage, Mike had been afraid for Jenny. Now, while he peeled off his wet clothes, had his bath and put on his pajamas, he suddenly found himself getting more and more afraid for himself and for Hilda.

He had seen Jenny looking helplessly down at him from the flaming hut and he had known that he could not save her. He had seen Dad's face in the moment before Jenny jumped. He had seen Mother's eyes on Jenny in that split second when Jenny lay crumpled up in her father's arms with her own eyes tightly closed.

Now he felt fear over again in himself, for all of it had been his fault. And as soon as the Macgregors thought about it, as soon as they looked at him and really saw him, they would send Hilda and him away.

If they had been adopted . . . but they were not. They were foster children. He knew a boy at school who had been in six foster homes before he was ten years old. Rodney had stolen things and told lies, but, as far as Mike knew, he had never been to blame for a fire.

"But I want to leave!" Mike told himself fiercely. "Why should I care?"

It was no comfort. Pop still had no place for them. Hilda was happy here. What would Pop say when he was told?

Suppose their next foster mother was like Aunt Dorrie! He could bear it — but what would happen to Hilda?

Mother was going out the door. He had scarcely spoken to her since they came upstairs together. She had stayed with him while he undressed and he had been ashamed to find himself trembling. It had taken him a long time to undo his shoelaces. But Mother had run more hot water into the tub, and when she came back into the room, he had managed to get them untied. She had gone away while he had his bath, only to reappear with a cup of hot chocolate just as he was buttoning his pajama top.

"Thanks," he said — and found that his voice was shaking too.

Mother did not seem to notice. "Sit down," she said, "and let me part your hair properly."

Mike collapsed onto a chair. He sipped obediently at his hot chocolate. He felt dazed. Mother slicked back his hair, and then the comb cut through it in a line as straight as a ruler.

"You won't be a prisoner here for long," Mother said, putting the comb back on the dresser and taking his empty cup from him. "Take it easy, Mike."

She left, giving him a smile over her shoulder before she closed the door firmly. It was then that Mike thought of Alec.

"He's a spy," he muttered savagely. "If he hadn't run and tattled . . ."

Mike did not let himself finish that thought. He could not settle anywhere. He scuffed around the room, kicking at the wastebasket, thrusting a chair out of his way with a bump of his knee. He knew he should be angry at Jenny, not Alec. Jenny had been the real spy. He had caught her red-handed, snooping around in his private hideout. But that was just it. Jenny had dared to go up there. He would have done that himself if he had discovered someone else's hut. She had been exploring — not just hiding and watching as Alec must have done.

There was a snuffling sound along the crack under the door.

"Good old Fleet," Mike said softly, but he did not let him in. After a minute, he heard the dog lying down outside — thump, thump, thump, one leg at a time.

Then somebody knocked. Mike dived for the bed and tried to look as though he had been stretched out there ever since Mother left.

"Come in," he called.

Dad pushed Jenny in ahead of him. If Mike had been angry with her, it would have been hard to stay angry once he saw her. Proud Jenny, Jenny who never called him Mike without taking a deep breath first, Jenny always so certain she was right, had been humbled. Her head was hanging down so that he could not see her face. Her barrette was missing and her dark hair flopped untidily into her eyes. When at last, she glanced up at him, he saw that she had been crying.

Mike was shocked. She had caught her finger in the car door on Sunday and she had just stood, her head high, her lips pressed tight.

"Ooh, Jenny, I'd cry," Hilda had said frankly.

And Jenny had answered loftily, "I'm not a baby."

Mike had seen her toss her head defiantly. He had seen her bite her lip or clench her fists. He had watched her blush and he had heard her sob, that once, just before she jumped into Dad's arms. But now her eyes were red and he could see a smear of tears still wet on her cheek.

He got up and moved over to stand beside her. (Fleet, who had come in on Dad's heels, ranged himself on Mike's other side.) The boy had no way of knowing about *The Birds' Christmas Carol.* He wondered, his stomach tightening, if she were that afraid of what Dad was going to do to them.

Dad talked. When Douglas Macgregor was angry, he had no trouble finding words. He told Mike how dangerous it had been to stretch that extension cord along the rafters as he had done. There could easily have been a fire without Jenny's having gone near the place. He said he did not need to tell Jenny that it was criminal to play with matches. Hadn't she been told that ever since she was a baby?

Jenny nodded, still not looking directly at either of them.

He asked if she had any excuse to offer. She shook her head mutely. Mike shook his too.

Dad's voice went on and on and on, talking about things they both knew already. Slowly, very slowly, Mike realized that Mr. Macgregor had no thought of sending either Hilda or himself away. There was no mention of "foster children." Rodney had been called "incorrigible" — he was proud of it — but Dad never used the word.

Instead he finished up by telling them how thankful they should both be that Alec had happened along.

At that, Jenny looked up. She even started to protest, but then she closed her mouth and left the words unsaid. Watching her, Mike understood how she at last had found his secret hideout. It was Alec. Alec had led her there when he knew Mike was safely out of the way. Jenny, now standing straight and facing her father, saw the awareness dawn in Mike's eyes.

"Alec," their glances said to each other. "It's Alec's fault. Without him, it never would have happened."

The lecture was blessedly over. Dad smiled at them and watched them smile feebly back. He rose and put a hand on each of their shoulders.

"Now let's forget about it and go have our supper," he said.

But neither Jenny nor Michael was ready to forget.

There was a punishment. It began the next day when Dad arrived home from work. Like all Dad's punishments, it fitted the crime. Mike and Jenny were to build a playhouse in the backyard. Dad brought home brand-new lumber, nails, everything they needed. They were to work together on it for at least two hours a day until it was done. They were not to leave the Macgregor yard until it was finished. And when it was finished, it was to be the property of Alec, Mac and Hilda. Neither of the older children was to be allowed inside.

If Dad had wanted to make Jenny accept Mike, he need not have bothered. Being in trouble together had made them allies. But having to build that playhouse was terrible. Dad planned it with Mike, and inspected regularly, so it had to be well done. But Jenny, who was awkward with tools, was forever hammering her thumb. The three younger children were underfoot every minute of the day, and Fleet did nothing but step in the nails or carry off the tools.

"I'm going to put my dolly's dishes in there and have parties," Hilda announced happily, when the shape of the house could be seen.

"Get back!" Mike roared at her. "I just about took your eye out with this hammer!"

"It's not a girl's house," Mac said, differing with Hilda for once. "It's a bunkhouse, like cowboys have."

"You're not the boss of it, Malcolm Macgregor!"

"Well, neither are you, so there! I'm as much boss as you are."

"Ladies get first choice." Hilda sounded smug.

"Ladies!! I don't see any lady around here."

Dad arrived on the scene and they ran to him for a decision. Alec was standing by, watching, not saying a word. Dad looked at him and frowned.

"Alec is going to be the boss of this playhouse," he told the younger ones suddenly. "He's the eldest and he should have the most sense. He'll see that you take fair turns. After all, if it hadn't been for him running to the rescue, you wouldn't have these two fine carpenters at work for you now."

Alec stuck out his chest and began to walk around the playhouse importantly. Jenny and Mike looked at each other and gritted their teeth.

12

Mr. Small's Mistake

A WEEK went by. The playhouse was nearly finished. The Jacksons had lived in their new "home" for a month. Then, one afternoon when everybody else was out, Mike and Dad had an adventure of their own.

Mike often thought how strange it was that all the others were somewhere else at that particular time. In that whole first month, he had never before, that he could remember, been alone in the house with Dad. But when Mother announced that Jenny, Hilda and Alec had to go to the dentist, Mac demanded to be taken along.

"And you can take us out to the Midway," he had added brightly. "That will make up for all the fillings and things."

"But how about you?" Mother had teased. "You had your teeth fixed in June. No fillings, no ride?"

Mac gave her an earnest, reproachful look, guaranteed to melt her heart.

"When they suffer, I suffer," he told her.

Mike was starting down the stairs when the door bell rang. He kept on coming as Dad crossed the hall to the door. But he stopped abruptly on the second-from-the-bottom step when a strange man's voice said, "Does a Michael Jackson live here?"

"Yes, he does," Dad said. "Mike!"

Mike went forward slowly. At any other time, Dad would

have called him and then left him alone with his visitor. Perhaps it was the hard note in this man's voice, perhaps it was the baffled look on Mike's face, but this time Dad stayed put.

"You're Michael Jackson?" the man asked.

Mike nodded.

"Yes, he's Mike Jackson," Dad agreed smoothly, "but neither of us knows you."

The man hesitated. He took another look at Dad.

"Aren't you Mr. Macgregor from the library?" he asked.

He was clearly bewildered at finding Mike living with the Macgregors. Dad stepped forward casually and laid an arm around Mike's shoulders. He did not hold the boy against himself or even pat him reassuringly, but he kept his arm there throughout the interview that followed.

"Yes, I am Douglas Macgregor — and this is my foster son, Michael Jackson. But, as I mentioned, we do not know your name."

Then the man explained. His name was Mr. Small. He was from the five-and-ten. That morning, Joey Webster, Nick Zarnoff and Henry Schmitt had been caught shoplifting in the store. They had been caught before and warned. This time a police officer had accompanied him to talk to their parents. Henry's young brother had told them about the boys' tree house and had even showed them where to find it.

"They wouldn't let him join their gang and he was mad," Mr. Small explained.

In the tree house, they had uncovered boxes full of stolen articles. They had also found two books with "Michael Jackson" written in them. And on the doorpost, four sets of initials had been carved. J.W., N.Z., M.J., and H.S.

"We asked who Michael Jackson was, and Joey told us that

you were involved in it with them. Henry agreed with him. He gave me this address. Nick did not say anything then, but when we talked to him alone, he said they were lying. We did not know whether he was telling the truth or whether he was protecting a friend. The police had no evidence against you, but I decided that your parents should know the sort of friends you have and the trouble you may be getting into."

Mr. Small was sounding friendlier, but Mike was too stunned to notice. He had carved his initials that spring. He

remembered the books, a couple of adventure stories. He was grateful to Nick for standing up for him, but would anyone believe Nick?

"Mike has not been involved in any such activities since we have known him," Dad said.

He looked down at Mike. He was remembering the day Mike had been missing, the battered boy who had come home after supper.

"As a matter of fact, I happen to know that he was not a

member of this gang any more than Henry's little brother,"
Dad went on, his voice strong and sure. "How old are these
boys? Fourteen? Fifteen?"

Mr. Small nodded. Mike gulped back a gasp of astonishment. How did Dad know about Joey, Henry and Nick?
How was he so certain Mike had not been stealing from the
five-and-ten? Mr. Small seemed to wonder about the same
things. He looked doubtful.

"Mike is eleven," Dad explained. "When you were fifteen,
did you take an eleven-year-old along with you when you
started out to do something you didn't want your mother to
know about?"

Mr. Small thought about it. He shook his head.

"Mike went over to his tree house about a month ago. He
came home looking exactly as though three boys, probably
Joey, Nick and Henry, had thrown him out on his ear. If you
had come here a week ago, I could still have shown you traces
of bruises. Since that time, he has not been allowed to leave
the property without accounting to either my wife or myself.
He has been building another 'hideout' to take the place of
the tree house. He has been a busy boy."

Mike waited for Dad to tell what happened to his new
hideout, but Dad did not say a word about the fire. He just
rested his hand a little more firmly on Mike's shoulder and,
looking straight at Mr. Small, said, "I appreciate your coming,
Mr. Small. But I vouch for Mike's whereabouts and for his
honesty. He's a good boy and I'm glad he has joined our
family."

There was nothing more Mr. Small could say.

"Well, sorry to have bothered you," he muttered as he
turned to leave.

"Not at all," Dad replied politely. But when he shut the door, it almost slammed.

Mike gathered his scattered wits and faced Dad.

"How did you know?"

"Oh, I just keep both eyes open, as Alec would say." Dad grinned at him. As he turned to go back to his book, he paused. "But Mike, I meant what I said," he remarked over his shoulder.

Left alone in the hall, Mike heard again, in his heart, what Dad had said. "He's a good boy and I'm glad he has joined our family."

"Boy, I'm glad Pop wasn't here," he thought suddenly.

He started back upstairs, forgetting that he had been about to go out and work on the playhouse. Not till he was alone in his room did he realize that, in being glad his father had not been there, he had been preferring Dad to Pop.

"But I love Pop!" he cried.

Still, a small, honest voice inside him persisted in being glad that Pop had been absent. Pop would have grown angry. Dad had been angry too, Mike recognized now, but when Pop was angry, he shouted.

"And would he have trusted me?" the small voice asked. Mike was not used to people trusting him so far that they were ready to vouch for his honesty.

At last he saw what his father had seen weeks before when he had come to visit them for the first time at the Macgregors'. It was not that Pop did not love him or that he did not love Pop. It was just that Pop did not really know him.

Long ago, before Mom had died, they had known each other. Then Pop, too, would have been sure of his honesty. But Aunt Dorrie had given them no chance to be close to one another. And anyway, Pop was not a listener. In one month, Dad had learned more about him than Pop had discovered in the last four years.

Fleet, sleeping in a patch of sunshine, yelped excitedly. Mike reached out and prodded him with his foot.

"Quit chasing dream rabbits, you crazy hound," he ordered.

Then he jumped to his feet and started for the stairs. He had meant to work on the playhouse. He WOULD work on the playhouse. No Mr. Nosey-Parker Small, no troubling thoughts of his own, would stop him.

He was hard at work before he thought about his two fathers again.

"Pop is Pop," he said, understanding himself perfectly. "And Dad is Dad. Dad knows me better now, but Pop remembers Mom just like I do. Pop remembers when I was a baby. I like to listen to him talk. . . . Being glad he wasn't here this aftenoon doesn't have a thing to do with it. Of course I love him. He's . . . Pop."

Fleet raced away with a piece of board Mike was about to use.

"Fleet — fetch it, boy!" he yelled. Fleet came lolloping back with it just as Mike had trained him to. The boy took the board, patted the dog and said self-righteously, "It's a good thing for you I came here, you dumb dog. You would have forgotten everything Michael ever taught you."

Fleet had made him feel as though he were somehow in partnership with the first Michael, as though the other boy had left him the job of keeping the great dog well-behaved. He had taught him three new tricks already.

"Hi!"

"Hiya, Mike."

"We rode on a Ferris wheel."

They were home. Fleet rushed to welcome them. Mike waved his hammer in a gay salute. Mother waved her purse at him in return. She looked as though she had enjoyed the Ferris wheel almost as much as Mac.

"Wait till Dad tells her about Mr. Small," the small voice warned. But Dad said nothing. He only mentioned the matter once more — in private, to Mike himself.

"I don't see that we need to tell anyone about Mr. Small's mistake," he said, stopping Mike on his way to bed. "When people make mistakes, the kindest thing to do is to forget them."

The fear of being sent away, which had taken possession of Mike whenever he or Hilda did something wrong, began to fade in the days that followed. He started enjoying his work on the playhouse and he found himself wishing that Jenny would stop looking at him whenever Alec annoyed her. As though she and he had made a secret resolution to hate Alec forever! Well, he hadn't. He could have managed nicely without Alec and his show-off ways, but he could manage with him too.

Then the hammer was lost. Dad bought a painting and he wanted to hang it. He went to the drawer where the tools were kept, but the hammer was missing.

"Mike, where's the hammer?" he called.

Mike was reading the comics.

"In the drawer," he answered, not even turning his head.

Dad came into the living room and looked at him.

"If it were in the drawer, I would not need to ask its whereabouts," he said coldly.

Mike, who had been sprawled on his stomach, sat up and faced Dad. He thought hard for a second. Then his face cleared.

"I remember putting it there," he said. "Somebody else must have borrowed it."

Dad raised his eyebrows and looked at the rest of them.

"Not me," Jenny said grumpily. "I hate that old hammer."

"I didn't take it."

"Neither did I."

"No, Doug, I haven't seen it either."

"Well, Alec," Dad said, "you must be the guilty party. Where's the hammer?"

There was a sudden pause.

"I didn't have it," Alec said loudly. "Mike didn't bring it in. I saw him. He just brought in the saw. Somebody must have stolen it!"

13

Two Against One

"WHY you little liar . . ." Mike began, outraged.

"All right, Mike. Easy does it," Dad warned. "I hereby appoint a search party. Nobody is excused. We'll probably find that Jenny couldn't stand whacking her thumb one more time and pitched the hammer in the garbage in self-defense."

They searched the house and then the yard. It was Dad who found a lopsided wooden boat lying on the grass with a half dozen nails scattered beside it. Hilda suddenly remembered seeing Alec out there banging away at it just before Mother called them in to supper. The hammer was gone.

Dad took Alec up to his room. This did nothing to cool the rage in both Michael's and Jenny's hearts. They were angry at Alec, angry at his tattling on them on the afternoon of the fire, angry at his poking into their rooms when they were away, angry at the way they could not seem to turn around without finding him standing nearby, watching them, angry at the lie he had told. It seemed to them that Dad's lecture was very short indeed, and although Alec did not come back downstairs again, he would have had to go to bed in less than an hour anyway. The two of them met in Mike's room.

"The nerve of him!" Jenny stormed. "Trying to put the blame on you when he knew perfectly well he was the one who took that hammer out."

"Yeah," Mike said menacingly. "I'd sure like to teach that kid . . ."

"And spying on us that day in the garage." Jenny was getting madder by the minute.

"Well," Mike faced facts reluctantly, "it was a good thing he ran for your father."

"If he hadn't taken me there in the first place, there would never have been a fire to tattle about," Jenny retorted.

Mike nodded slowly. That made sense. The more he thought of it, the more it seemed as though all the trouble he had been in was Alec's fault. Jenny did not know about Mr. Small's visit. Mike did not tell her now. But he could not forgive Alec for lying about the hammer. Until the truth was discovered, Mike had been beset again by the old fear of being sent away. And added to it had been his certainty that Dad, who had been so sure of his honesty, now would no longer trust him. As he listened to Jenny going on and on about Alec's awfulness, Mike knew that she was exaggerating, that Alec was only nine, that he could not be the villian Jenny was picturing.

Then he thought of that one lie, and his heart hardened.

"What will we do to him?" he asked.

"I have part of an idea," Jenny said thoughtfully. "Wait til tomorrow."

The next morning, at breakfast, they were given their allowances. Mac and Hilda immediately rushed out the front door. They loved popsicles, and they had started, two weeks before, to buy each flavor in turn so that they could make up their minds which was the best.

"Let's have blueberry this time," Hilda's voice drifted back.

Mother shuddered and began clearing the table. Soon the three of them were alone in the dining room.

"Hey, Alec," Jenny said casually, "do you want to play with Mike and me?"

Alec turned from watching the door swing shut behind Mac and Hilda.

Later, Jenny was to remember exactly how he looked at her. He eyed her suspiciously, as though he did not believe she meant it. Then, in spite of himself, his face lit up.

"What are you going to do?" he wanted to know.

That was Alec all over. They should have known he would never say yes without checking first. Mike was not prepared for the question, but Jenny answered smoothly, "We're going to play circus and we want three people. Maybe we'll use Fleet too," she added, inspired.

"Well . . ." Alec said slowly, trying to keep the happiness out of his voice. "Okay. I guess so." The three of them went out into the yard. When Fleet tried to follow them, Jenny shut the door on him. "Not yet," she told him. "You'll get into everything."

The playhouse stood there, practically finished. Mike looked slantwise at Jenny and then squared his shoulders and started to whistle through his teeth. Jenny was watching the grass in front of her. Alec, who always listened and waited, who let others do the suggesting, suddenly said:

"Fleet could be a lion, and I could be a lion tamer."

They had passed the playhouse. They had reached the corner farthest from the house. Jenny looked over her shoulder to make sure they were out of sight of the kitchen windows. Then she reached out and grabbed her younger brother roughly by one shoulder.

"What's the matter?" Alec burst out in a startled rush.

"You're a liar and a tattletale and a sneak, that's what's the matter," Jenny spat at him.

Mike, who had begun to wonder whether this was a good idea, grew angry all over again at Jenny's outburst.

"I told you," he growled at Alec. "I warned you. I said 'Stay out of my things.' But oh no! Not such a little sneak as you are! You don't even care if your sister burns to death."

The eagerness had vanished from Alec's face. He stared back at them, his eyes hard, his jaw set. Jenny thought afterwards that if, right then, he had mumbled he was sorry or let tears come into his eyes or even hung his head and looked ashamed, they would not have gone on with it. But Alec did none of these things. He kept his head high and he looked at them coldly.

"You're liars yourselves saying you want to play circus," he said scornfully. "And it's a good thing I tattled to Dad for you. Next time you need him, I won't bother."

They tied him up. They bound his ankles together and then tied his wrists behind him. Then they made him lie down and Jenny held him still while Mike fastened the two ropes together. Alec still did not care, or if he did, he gave no sign.

"I'll tell," he said calmly when Jenny stood up and they looked down at him, bent up and helpless at their feet.

They gagged him then, with a big handkerchief Mike had. But still he stared boldly back at them without flinching.

"We'll go away and leave you here until you learn not to be such a sneak," Jenny told him. That was as far as her plans went, but his eyes answered that it did not matter to him. He would be rescued eventually. Then, whatever she said or did, he would tell, and they would be punished.

Jenny could not stand it. A mean little baby like Alec, despising her! . . . Suddenly, savagely, she wanted to hurt him, to make him admit, once and for all, that she was the stronger.

"I know what we'll do to you since you think you're so smart," she said softly, slowly, her voice shocking in its cruelty. "We'll put worms on you. . . ."

Mike looked at her, amazed by what she had said, but Jenny was watching her small brother. She saw him stiffen with horror, just as she had known he would.

"Worms and caterpillars and . . . a spider, if I can find one," she went on, almost dreamily. "That will teach you, won't it, Alec?"

"There's a caterpillar," Mike said blankly. He still had no clear idea of what was happening.

"Bring it here," Jenny commanded.

Mike came with a pretty little fuzzy green caterpillar cupped in his palm. Taking it from him, Jenny really saw it for a fraction of a second, saw its minute feelers waggling busily, saw its soft green bristles, felt the dry tickling feeling of it crawling across her hand.

Then she reached down to put it on Alec's bare arm.

"Jenny," Mother called from the house. "Jenny! Mike! Go see if you can find them, Mac."

They jumped guiltily. The caterpillar dropped, unheeded, from Jenny's hand.

"Come on," she whispered urgently. "We'll come back. We can't let Mac find us."

Leaving Alec a prisoner behind the bushes, they raced off to the house.

14

Jenny Understands

MAC was nowhere to be seen. The two of them crossed the lawn at a run and found Mother standing at the screen door.

"What is it?" Jenny puffed.

"Come in and see for yourselves." Mother stood back and let them pass.

There sat Hildy, with a wan face and an important air.

"Mother thinks I broke my arm, Mike," she announced proudly. "I was chasing Mac and I tripped because of my shoelace being loose and my shoe started to come off and I couldn't stop myself and I fell down the front steps and did it ever hurt! Look! See how fat it is!"

She lifted her arm gingerly and displayed a badly swollen wrist.

"I always say if you want excitement, come to the Macgregors' when it is holiday time and the dear children are all at home starting fires, shutting car doors on themselves, and whacking their thumbs with hammers, breaking their wrists and so on." Mother's voice was rueful and amused at the same time.

"Gosh!" Mike said. He looked at his small plump sister with respect.

"Mac says I'm the only one in this family ever to break a bone," Hilda bragged, laying her arm back on the table very gently.

Only Mother noticed that, to Hilda, Mac's family was now hers.

"Dad is coming home from the library to take her up for an X-ray in just a few minutes," she told the older children. "But she wanted to show you, Mike, before she went. I wonder if you'd run over to the garage and tell your father what has happened. I tried to get him, but the line is out of order or something. Tell him we'll let him know the results of the X-ray as soon as we know ourselves."

"Sure," Mike said.

"You tell him I didn't even cry . . . hardly even, that is," Hilda instructed. "And tell him it is really broken and that I am the first one in the whole family to have a broken bone. . . ."

"Okay, okay," Mike protested.

"It may interest you to know, Miss Hilda Mary Jackson, that I broke my ankle when I was eight," Mother said with a smile.

Hilda looked at Mother. She clearly found it hard to believe, that once upon a time Mother had been eight years old.

"How did you do it?" Jenny asked. She had never heard this story before.

Mike halted in the doorway, waiting to hear too.

Mother looked embarrassed all at once. Then she grinned at them.

"Well, you see, it was this way," she told them. "It was the summer holidays and my brother Gregory dared me to jump off the porch roof, using an umbrella for a parachute."

"Mo-ther!" Jenny gasped. "You didn't DO it?"

"Didn't I?" Mother shook her head over her young reckless

self. "But when I dared Gregory, the next day, he was a sissy and wouldn't even try."

Mike left, bent over with laughter. Jenny leaned closer and looked admiringly at Hilda's wrist.

"What will the doctor do to it, Mother?" she asked.

"He'll put a cast on it, and I imagine she'll have to wear it up in a sling for a while. She's going to need your help, Jenny. It is her right hand. She is going to have trouble dressing and eating and doing all sorts of things until the bone knits. I have a feeling that our Hildy is going to be one thankful little girl on the day her cast is removed."

"I'm thirsty," Hilda said. She sounded as though she wanted to cry. "I'm thirsty," she repeated loudly.

Jenny knew that she was more frightened than thirsty but she went for some lemonade.

"Put an ice cube in it," Mother said. "Then why don't you sit and play a game of Chinese checkers with her, Jenny, until your father arrives. That will give her practice using that left hand."

Hilda brightened when Jenny fetched the Chinese checker board.

"Let's play 'space jump,'" she said.

She even laughed as her marbles got knocked out of place and rattled their way wildly across the board. Before they knew it Mike was back.

"Pop wasn't there," he said.

"Where was he?" Hilda asked, the tremor back in her voice. "I want him."

"He had a couple of days off and he went up north with Mr. Masters. I think they went fishing," Mike told her.

It was hard for him to accept too. Never before could he think of a time when Pop had gone out of town without telling them all about it first.

But before he could reassure himself or his sister, Mac brought Alec in. The moment she saw Alec, Jenny knew that she had done a wicked thing. Mac looked like the older brother. He had one of Alec's arms across his shoulders and his own arm was around Alec's waist, steadying him. Alec was leaning on Mac, as though he could not stand alone, but Mac was standing bolt upright, in spite of Alec's weight. He was scarlet with rage.

"I found him, Mother," he got out. "Jenny and Mike had tied him up and gagged him and left him out there, so he couldn't hardly move. And Jenny put a caterpillar right on his neck. She knows he's scared of bugs and stuff, but she did it on purpose. She put it right on him and . . ."

"All right, Mac. Hush now," Mother said. She did not look at Mike or Jenny. She simply pulled up the nearest chair, sat down and took Alec on her lap. As soon as her arms closed around him, he started to cry as though he would never stop, with his face pressed tightly against her shoulder. Mac pushed up close to the two of them and patted Alec's arm comfortingly. Even Hilda had forgotten her broken wrist as she looked at Alec. Her eyes were wide with astonishment and pity.

"But I didn't put that caterpillar on his neck!" Jenny defended herself silently. "I just . . . I just dropped it . . . and I was standing right beside him . . ."

You could see the marks on his bare legs and on his wrists where he had fought to get free. His clothes were grass-stained. There was a bit of grass still caught in his hair. His

face was hidden now, but Jenny had seen it. His lips looked burned from twisting to get the gag off, and his eyelids were swollen with crying.

She and Mike stood very still watching. There was no way they could comfort Alec. There was no way they could excuse themselves.

Suddenly, Alec began to shiver. With one hand, he reached around and grabbed at the back of his shirt.

"I can still feel them, Mummy," he gasped. "I can feel them crawling on me."

As she listened, Jenny felt them too. She, who had never minded holding any bug, in that instant knew what horror it must be to feel small dry feet inching across your bare back while you lay helpless. She glanced at Mike quickly. His eyes mirrored what she had felt.

Mother stood up and took off Alec's shirt. She shook it. She brushed off his back with the palm of her hand. There was no bug, not even an ant, there — but nobody told Alec to stop being silly.

"How about a bath?" Mother suggested as he still twisted his head around trying to see between his shoulder blades. She got up and took his hand. At last, she looked at Jenny and Mike.

"I would like you both to stay here until I come back," she said.

Mac gave them a look which said as plainly as any words, "Now you're going to get it!" But Jenny was watching Alec. He clung to Mother's hand. He had not once seemed aware of her and Mike. He did not see them now.

The front door opened.

"Where's the wounded heroine?" Dad called cheerfully.

Hilda slid off her chair, holding her arm out in front of her. She went to meet him, Alec forgotten. Mother and the two small boys followed. Jenny and Michael were left alone in the kitchen.

They heard Mother speaking quietly to Dad for a minute. They heard Dad exclaiming at the sight of Hilda's arm. They heard the car pull away. They heard Alec's bathwater running.

"It wasn't your fault . . . about the caterpillar, I mean," Jenny broke the silence between them. "You didn't know how scared he is of them."

"No," Mike agreed. After a pause, he added, "But really I did know though before we left. I could tell by the way he looked. And I didn't stop you. I didn't think you put it on his neck though."

"I didn't," Jenny said dully. "I must have just dropped it when I heard Mother calling. I didn't wait to see where it fell. It could have landed on his neck. I guess it must have. But I didn't do it on purpose."

From upstairs, they heard Mother say, "Now you look more like yourself. Why don't you two go outside and play for a while?"

"Come on, Alec," Mac urged, his voice warm with affection. "Let's take Michael's old football over to the park. Come on, old buddy."

It was then that Jenny understood. She knew in a flash what had seemed so familiar and yet so surprising when she had seen her little brothers standing together at the kitchen door.

"Where's Mac and Alec?" people had always asked. As though the two boys were one. As though they were certain that wherever one was, the other would be found. When Mac had gone adventuring, Alec had always followed, doing his level best to keep his brother out of trouble. They used to be always fighting, Jenny remembered, and Alec always won because Mac could not stay mad. Just when you knew that they were sworn enemies, you would come upon them building a snow fort or down on their knees playing marbles, as though they had never said an angry word to each other.

But now there was Hilda; Hilda, who was just Mac's age but who seemed younger; Hilda, who thought Mac was big and wonderful; Hilda, who wanted to be wherever Mac was and to do whatever he suggested. Now people talked about "Mac and Hildy," and now Alec was left by himself. The spy, the tattletale, the liar was only her little brother who had been lonely but too proud to ask for friendship.

Jenny all at once remembered a day long before. She had been feeling sorry for herself and she had thought, "I'm the only one who is alone. Alec and Mac have each other and Mother and Dad belong together. Always I have had Michael, but now I have nobody." Now she had Mike, Mac had Hilda, and Alec had nobody.

Mother stood in the doorway. They had been sitting, Mike perched on the tabletop and Jenny very straight on one of the chairs. They rose and faced her.

"I cannot talk to you about what you have done." Her voice was brittle and she looked at them as though they were strangers. "If you are making excuses for yourselves, I do not want to hear them. I have always thought that a certain amount of squabbling was natural in a family this size and I never worried about it. I hoped I had taught you that, underneath all the daily fighting and feuding, you must keep kind and loving hearts. Today I have to face the knowledge that I have failed. I don't know what more to do. If you decide you deserve to be punished, this time you will have to punish yourselves."

She turned on her heel and left them staring after her.

15

Mike Makes Peace

MIKE waited for Jenny to say something first.

At last, when she did not speak, he looked at her directly. She had not moved from the spot where she had stood to face Mother. She looked as though her mother had struck her with something harder than a few words. He could hear her breathing, funny little gasps of breath which frightened him. She was dry-eyed, but she looked so lost and lonely that Mike hastily looked away again.

"Hey, Jen, it's not that bad!" he said to her gruffly.

She did not answer.

Mike had a strong desire to leave her there. He was sorry about Alec too, but he was not all that sorry. Alec was fine now, wasn't he! It had not been so very long that they had left him out there in the first place. He would soon forget about it. Mike had had worse things happen to him, and he knew already that the worst of them became unimportant much sooner than you imagined it would.

Right now, he thought, Jenny was feeling far more upset than Alec. It had something to do with Mother. He did not understand what was wrong, but in the weeks he had lived in this house, he had seen Jenny flinch when Mother only said, "Do hurry up, Jenny!" or, "Keep those shoulders back. Your posture is dreadful."

"What Jenny needs is to have to live with Aunt Dorrie for a while," he told himself, and a grin turned up the corners of his mouth in spite of himself.

He hoped Jenny had not seen him smile, for part of him longed, even now, to bring her comfort. She reminded him of a pigeon with a broken wing which he had once found. Mom had let him keep it in a box in the kitchen and he thought it was beginning to trust him when it had died.

But the bird had been silly too. He had rescued it from the playground at school. He had come home early and risked Pop getting mad at him just to save it. He had made it a soft nest in the cardboard carton and he had tried to coax bread and milk into it with an eyedropper. And yet, in spite of his obvious love for it, in spite of his gentle care, its heart had pounded wildly whenever he touched it and it had hurt itself struggling to get away from him.

"Just like Jenny," Mike said to himself in exasperation.

Every day, Mother showed her love for Jenny in a hundred ways. But let her grow impatient and snap even once — that was what Jenny remembered! He still wanted to comfort her, but an even bigger part of him was itching to shake some sense into her.

"You should have seen Mother's face when she thought you were hurt the day of the fire," he almost shouted aloud. "You should have heard how worried she was about you that first time we went to the quarry."

But you couldn't make someone who looked the way Jenny did see sense.

"We could really have that circus, you know," he said finally, swinging himself up onto the table again and kicking his feet back and forth.

Jenny turned her head slowly and looked at him as though she had only just realized that he was still there.

"What?" she said.

"You know!" he snorted impatiently, swinging his legs hard enough to make the table jiggle and rattle. "That circus you told him we were going to have. Aw, come on, Jenny, wake up or I'm leaving. You . . . told . . . Alec . . . we were . . . going . . . to play . . . circus!"

He emphasized each word as though she did not understand English, and then Jenny remembered. He saw her remember. She was remembering all of it; the way Alec had wanted to be a lion-tamer, the way they had tied him up and gagged him, the things she had said and the voice she had used.

"If you're going to stand there and look like a sick cat, I'm quitting right now," Mike snapped.

He started to slide forward but Jenny put out her hand. He paused.

"You mean . . . really have a circus . . . and really let him be in it . . ." she asked, trying to take in the idea.

Mike sat back. All at once, he began to enjoy himself. Better than anything else, he loved planning things — tree houses, hideouts, circuses . . .

"Sure," he told her. "We could have a giant. He could sit on my shoulders, see, and we could put on a long coat of your dad's over both of us. His head and arms would show, and my legs. I saw some kids do that once. We could have a trained dog act, if we could get Fleet to do something. How about it, hound?"

"He's not a hound," Jenny said automatically. Fleet, who

had been feeling miserable with them for the last hour, brightened and thumped the floor with his tail.

Color came back into Jenny's cheeks. She started to look like herself again. She even reached up and shoved her hair-clip into place. She did this a hundred times a day, Mike was sure, without even knowing she did. He was pleased with himself.

"Could we have it this afternoon? It's Wednesday and Dad will be home. We could make them buy tickets and come."

"Sure. And Mac can be a bareback rider. I'll be the horse," Mike explained, laughing now. "And maybe we could use Michael's stilts. They're in the garage."

"Let's go ask Alec," Jenny said, suddenly brave. "Let's find him and ask him right away."

Then her face clouded with doubt.

"Do you think he will . . . after what we . . ."

"Of course he will. Don't be silly. Come on." Mike led the way. Alec and Mac were in the yard throwing the ball back and forth. Alec saw them coming and missed the pass Mac shot at him. Mac glared openly.

"Keep away from us, you big bullies," he shouted.

Jenny stopped in her tracks, but Mike just grinned down at the ruffled little boy.

"Calm down and shut up," he told him good-naturedly. "We have an idea."

"Who cares?" Mac flashed back.

"You might if you'd listen for two seconds."

At the word "circus," they both saw Alec stiffen. "Alec, we're sorry," Mike appealed to him. His face and tone of voice were both so sincere that a little of Alec's wariness went.

"We didn't plan to leave you there and Jenny didn't even know where she dropped that crazy caterpillar. We felt sorry as soon as we saw you, and to top things off, now your mother isn't speaking to either of us. This time, we really mean it though . . . about having a circus. We could all be in it and we could even charge admission."

He described some of the ideas for circus acts that he and Jenny had already had. Before he finished, Mac's eyes were glowing with excitement and even Alec was looking quietly pleased. There was no need to talk any longer about whether or not they would do it. The four of them drifted over to the veranda steps to plan.

When Hilda came out through the door from the living room, they were so absorbed that it was a moment before they noticed her.

"Look," she said. "Mike, look at me."

They crowded around her, examining the sling, reaching out to touch the plaster cast.

"You can all write your names on it," she promised, beaming at them. "The doctor said I was the bravest girl he ever saw. He gave me a jelly bean, a black one. I saved it for you, Jenny. I didn't tell him I hate black ones."

"She can be in the circus," Mike said suddenly to the others. "She can be a freak. The Girl with the Plaster Arm!"

"Yeah," they agreed joyfully.

"What circus?" asked Hilda.

Talking all at once, they told her.

16

The Willful Lamb

JENNY made the posters. She used Alec's colored markers and made them as gay and as exciting as she could.

COME ONE!   COME ALL!!
SEE THE WORLD FAMOUS
MACGREGOR-JACKSON CIRCUS!!
SEE THE 10 FOOT TALL GIANT!
SEE THE GIRL WITH THE PLASTER ARM!
SEE FEARLESS FERDINAND, THE DEATH DEFYING
LION-TAMER!!
SEE THE BAREBACK RIDER!   SEE THE CLOWN!
3 O'CLOCK   ADULTS 15¢
MACGREGOR'S YARD   CHILDREN 5¢
PROCEEDS FOR HUMANE SOCIETY   BABIES FREE

She was very proud of them when they were finished. She hurried to show them to Mike. But he was much too busy to stop and admire them.

"Go stick them up," he commanded. "One of them on the tree in front and a couple up the street. Ask Mr. Neal if you can put one in the drugstore."

Jenny did as she was told. Without Mike, there would be no circus. She had never seen him like this before. He had all of them hustling around getting things ready. They had found an old brown blanket with which to turn Mike into a horse. Mac was making himself a bareback rider's costume out of Hilda's leotards. They had to be pinned. Sturdy boy though he was, he was only half her width. Mike and Alec were building a circus ring.

"You have to be the clown," Mike told Jenny when she came running back.

"The clown!" Jenny wailed. "Mike, I can't!"

"You have to. All the rest of us have something else to do and you wrote SEE THE CLOWN! on your posters."

"But how . . ."

"You figure it out," he said offhandedly, turning away from her to answer a shout from Mac.

Jenny went into the house and began to search for the clown costume. Michael had been a clown in a play once, she was sure — but did they still have any of Michael's things? She went up to the Odds-and-Ends room. It was a small storeroom, its many cupboards and boxes crammed with clothes which were outgrown or out of season. There were also piles of suitcases, photograph albums, and in the midst of everything else Mother's sewing machine. Mother kept trying to call it the sewing room, but nobody else bothered.

Jenny found dozens of interesting things but no costume meant for a clown. She sat on the floor and began on the bottom drawers.

Mother came in with a torn pajama top of Alec's in her hand. She was whistling softly. She did not see Jenny at once. Jenny recognized Hilda's song.

> *The shepherds had an angel,*
> *The Wise Men had a star,*
> *But what have I. . . .*

"Well," Mother said, catching sight of Jenny all at once. "One of my willful lambs!"

Jenny looked blank. Then it came to her. It was from the same song.

> *The lambs lie in his bosom*
> *Along life's dangerous track;*
> *The willful lambs who go astray*
> *He, bleeding, fetches back.*

Perhaps Mother, too, thought of the words, for her face grew kinder all at once. She almost smiled.

"What in the world are you doing?" she asked

"We're having a circus . . ." Jenny began.

"A circus," Mother interrupted. Her face grew stern again. Jenny realized that Alec must have told her how they had pretended they were going to play circus earlier. Told how *she* had pretended really, for Mike had only followed her lead. She felt herself blushing deeply. She could not think of words to go on with.

"Who is your lion-tamer?" Mother said quietly.

"Alec," Jenny managed.

"Good for you." Mother really smiled this time, a warm smile that lighted the morning, which, to her daughter, had seemed so dark just a little while before.

"But, darling," she went on, her eyes puzzled, "what are you burrowing into the winter clothes for?"

"I have to be a clown. Mike says I have to, but I can't find the costume . . . and I don't know how to do it either."

"Well, I know where the costume is," Mother said. She opened one of the cupboards, reached down a big suit box and opened it. It was packed full of clothes. With a shock, Jenny recognized them — Michael's gray pants, his plaid lumberjack shirt, his blazer, and in with the rest the clown suit. Mother lifted it out and tried to shake the creases out of it.

Then, under the clothing, Jenny caught sight of Michael's Yo-Yo. And glancing up at the shelf from which Mother had taken the box, she saw the box which held their butterfly collection, the box she had always imagined Mother had thrown away. Mother hung the clown costume over a chair, closed the big box, shoved it back up onto the shelf, and turning, saw the look on Jenny's face.

"Jenny," she said, gently, "what is it?"

"You have Michael's things," Jenny explained carefully. Tears began to run down her cheeks. She did not know why. Already she knew that she had been wrong, that Mother missed Michael just as much as she did, that Mother loved them both as she always had. But she could not stop the tears.

Mother sat down and drew Jenny up from the floor. She held her close.

"Jenny, darling, it's all right," she murmured softly, kissing Jenny's wet cheek. "Tell me."

"I thought . . . I thought sometimes . . . that I was the only one who missed him," Jenny gulped. "I even thought you didn't want me to care about him any more. . . ."

"I see." Mother rested her chin on top of Jenny's head. "And I see that I made a mistake. Jenny, I want to tell you why I made it." She paused as though she were gathering her words together.

"I have often told you about the months I spent with my Aunt Marie when I was your age, haven't I," she began quietly. "But I never mentioned — at least I don't remember mentioning — Aunt Marie's son Edward."

Jenny was mystified. What on earth could Mother's Aunt Marie's son Edward have to do with it?

"Aunt Marie was my mother's sister, but she was much older than Mother. She was about twenty when Mother was born. By the time Mother was ten, Aunt Marie had married Uncle Jason and had had one son, Edward. Edward was my first cousin, but he was sixteen when I was born. He died when I was three."

"Oh," Jenny said blankly. Maybe there was some connection after all. But how could there be if Mother was only three when this Edward died?

"Aunt Marie had always taken immense pride in Edward. He went to the best schools. He wore the most expensive clothes. He had lessons of all kinds: riding, fencing, elocution. She planned to make him into a famous lawyer.

"When I went to stay with her — Mother was sick and the doctor prescribed a long rest — Aunt Marie never let me forget Edward for a moment, even though he had been dead for eight years. You couldn't move in that house without running into 'Cousin Edward's Ghost.' The bookcases were full of his books. His umbrella still stood in the hall stand. The clock on his desk had never been wound since the day he died. His clothes still hung in his closet and nobody ever stayed in his room."

"I would have been scared to," Jenny commented.

"So would I," Mother said. "Aunt Marie was forever telling me about his last sickness and his tragic death. But not once, Jenny, did she speak of gay things he had done or happy times they had shared. Mother, who had liked him, used to try and tell Gregory and me about the person he really was.

But his umbrella, his razor which was still in the bathroom, all his things were more alive to us than Edward was. When at last I went home after six months, I hoped I would never hear his name again as long as I lived."

"I don't blame you," Jenny put in sympathetically.

"Jenny, after Michael was killed, I thought, 'I must never let our memories of Michael grow to be the burden that Edward's memory became.' I imagined you sitting brooding over the accident and cherishing Michael's things as though they were more important than Michael himself."

Jenny understood now, understood the long misunderstanding. It was as though the sun had come out from behind a dark bank of cloud.

"I still think I was right in part," Mother defended herself. "Moving Alec into Michael's room, changing your places at the table, putting most of Michael's things out of sight . . . made living easier. But I should have explained. I don't think the boys miss Michael in any way they can talk about. But I should have known — I don't see how I could not have known — that you needed help and comfort. As a matter of fact, I have realized it lately but I wasn't sure how to begin. You never said anything at all. . . ."

Both of them sat, for a moment, remembering all the times they had wanted to speak, all the things they had almost said — and Jenny, as well as her mother, saw that part of the blame for the diffidence which had come between them was hers.

"I miss Michael too, Jenny," Mother said at last. "Sometimes the whole world seems empty without him."

Jenny took a deep breath and plunged in, facing fears she

had not admitted even to herself before and holding none of them back. "Sometimes, Mother, I feel awful — not because I'm lonely for him — but because I get so happy and busy, I forget all about him. For a whole day even! I love him so much — how can I forget?"

"Suppose you had been the one who was killed that day. Would you have wanted Michael to sit and think about you and be lonely every minute for the rest of his life? Stop and really remember him, Jenny. Remember the fun he had, the way he put every inch of himself into living each moment."

Mother's voice was husky, and Jenny saw that now she was not the only one with tears in her eyes.

"Just when I think I can't bear it without Michael, Mac will say something funny or Hilda will spill out one of her long wonderful speeches and I have to laugh. And when I am laughing at them or when I am busy, I don't think of Michael either. But I don't stop loving him just because he isn't in my thoughts for a while. And neither do you, darling. Wherever we go and whatever we do, we will always remember and love him."

She picked up the clown costume and held it up for Jenny to see.

"Remember Michael as a clown?" she asked, with a shaky chuckle.

Jenny cuddled closer to her and shook her head happily.

"Oh that's right. You were at your Aunt Amy's. He was in the Sunday school concert and he was supposed to sing a song about what a gay life a clown led. Bobby Shafer dared him to sing something else, and between them they cooked up a new set of words. He was supposed to sing:

> *The life of a clown is a merry life.*
> *All clowns are gay and glad.*
> *I'm a clown and, as you can see,*
> *I'm a jolly sort of lad.*
>
> *I sing and prance and laugh and play.*
> *My suit's not very neat,*
> *But I don't care because I have*
> *A pair of dancing feet.*

"I remember. I remember," Jenny cried, sitting up, her eyes shining, her tears vanished away. "I saw him practice. He made up crazy words and everybody clapped like mad, didn't they, and even Mrs. Hollister had to forgive him. I think I even remember the song."

"Let's hear you try it," Mother said.

Jenny sang with a long face:

> *The life of a clown is a dismal life,*
> *Always glum and sad.*
> *I'm a clown and, as you can see,*
> *I'm not a merry lad.*
>
> *Sometimes I try to sing and dance,*
> *But I've got such big feet,*
> *That every time I take a step,*
> *I end up on my seat.*

"Jenny Macgregor, that's perfect," Mother said. She pushed Jenny off her lap and laughed at her. "You sing that song every bit as well as Michael. You can so be a clown. I'll bet you can even do the little dance. Come on out in the hall and we'll see."

Hope filled Jenny's heart — hope and a wonderful airy peace.

"Okay," she said. "Okay, let's."

17

Ladeez and Gentlemen!

THE circus began promptly at three. They had put up arrows pointing to the side gate where Mike took in the money. Most of the children were Mac's and Hilda's age or younger, but Roger and Susan Hamilton, who had just arrived home that morning, came. Several mothers accompanied their children and Mike jingled the nickels and dimes gleefully. Alec escorted Mother and Dad out the front door and around by the gate so that they had to pay just like everyone else.

The children sat on the grass and the grown-ups took the chairs which had been placed in a row for them at the end of the yard. Mike was Ringmaster. He had on an old black coat of Mother's which hung almost to his ankles. He had turned the sleeves inside out to make it look like a proper cape and every time he tried to make it swirl importantly, he practically lost it.

"Ladeez and gentlemen," he bellowed impressively, flourishing his cape, and then clutching at it as it slipped, "in this very ring, right before your eyes, you are going to be privileged to see Fearless Ferdinand with his wild animal act. This is Ferdinand's only performance in Canada. He is known throughout the world for his daring and skill. This beast is a ferocious man-eater but Ferdinand can make him sit on a box, jump over a stick and fetch a ball. This animal has devoured seven grown men and two children!"

A couple of the smallest children squealed with terror and excitement, but one of the older boys scoffed, "Aw, I'll bet it's only Fleet."

Alec came out of the garage. He was dressed in his swimming trunks and wearing his gun and holster. Like any good lion-tamer, he had a chair in one hand. With the other, he was keeping a tight grip on Fleet's leash. But this Fleet was quite a different animal from the Fleet of every day. Fastened around his neck to make him look like a lion, he had an old fur neckpiece, that had belonged to an aunt of Dad's. This was one lion who hated his mane. For the first time in his life, Fleet really and truly did seem ferocious as he leaped around wildly, snarling at the fox tails that dangled and swung under his nose.

Alec kept coming bravely, dragging his lion after him. At last they reached the ring which he and Mike had made earlier. It was not a ring in the strict sense of the word, but it was just what they needed. It had only three sides formed by setting the picnic table and the picnic benches on edge. The side facing the audience was left open. They entered the ring from the front and they made quick costume changes behind the table.

Alec put down the chair with a little grunt of relief and began trying to get Fleet to jump up on the box they had placed there for him. Fleet reared back and growled at his mane.

"Come on, Fleet. Up, boy!" Alec begged.

All at once Fleet decided he might be able to run away from the fur. He scrambled over the box in a mad dash, and then looked down to see whether it was still waving beneath

his chin. Everybody clapped happily. A lion jumping over a box was just as good as a lion perching on top of one.

The applause was too much for Ferdinand's wild beast. Fox neckpiece and all, he flew over the nearest picnic bench and vanished under the veranda. Dad, laughing till he shook, went to try to rescue him while Mike hissed at Alec, "Bow, Ferdinand, bow!"

Ferdinand giggled and bowed. Mike the Ringmaster ushered him out of the ring, explaining solemnly to the audience:

"No need for alarm, folks. Just keep your seats. The lion has only escaped temporarily. When he is captured, he will be as gentle as . . . a dog. Next, all look this way and see the bravest bareback rider of all time, Mac the Magnificent!"

Mac, dressed and ready, was waiting behind the picnic table with Mike's "horse" blanket. Mike ducked in with him, shed his cape, and with the blanket draped over him and pinned under his chin, went charging into the ring on all fours. He was bucking and rearing beautifully like a real unbroken colt from the Wild West. Mac followed with a swagger and set to bronco-busting "Danger."

"Whoa there, Danger," he said. He tried to look serious and menacing, but his face broke into a grin. Danger slowed down momentarily. Mac climbed on. He was instantly thrown. Danger bucked cheerfully. Mac the Magnificent got to his feet and approached him warily. With a sudden leap, he was back on top of Mike.

"All right now, you old Danger," he yelled in his high little-boy voice. "You get one more chance. I said I was a-gonna ride ya and, by thunder, I'm a-gonna do it too!"

The audience howled with laughter. They clapped wildly when Mac stood up very slowly and balanced precariously while Mike crawled around the ring. Then horse and rider disappeared. A second later Ringmaster Mike was back, a little out of breath, a little red in the face, but as swashbuckling as ever.

Jenny was next. The foolishness of the others had made her feel so silly and gay that she had to stand and concentrate on what a small sad clown she was before she shuffled out into the ring. She had on Dad's biggest shoes and her feet looked enormous. She could hardly manage to walk without one foot knocking into the other.

She stood and stared sadly at the children and grown-ups gathered before her. Mother had made her a big false nose and used lipstick to make her mouth droop pathetically. When the people were quiet and ready, she began to sing, her voice low and wistful. Toward the end of the song, she tried to dance, tripped over her own feet, and landed sprawled on her behind as the song finished. The applause was music to her ears.

As she got up and started off to help the giant get ready, she darted a look at Mother. Mother smiled a special smile, and nodded approval. Then Jenny saw Dad reach over and take Mother's hand. She had reminded them of Michael, but she could see that they were glad to be reminded.

Mac took the place of announcer.

"Ladeez and Gentlemen," he imitated Mike. "Step right this way to the Freak House. Don't all try to get in at once. Line up, if you please. No pushing. No shoving. See the Giant Ten Feet Tall and the Girl with the Plaster Arm!"

Inside the garage, which had been hastily cleaned up by piling things even higher and leaving a clear space right through the middle, the giant stood, or rather, leaned. He wore Dad's winter overcoat. He had Alec's head and arms, and away down at the bottom, Mike's legs. Near the giant, Hildy sat with her arm on display. Anybody who wanted to could autograph her cast. Everybody did. Children too little to write scribbled importantly, and then looked proudly at their "names."

As the audience came into the yard again, Mac showed them out, walking along beside them on Michael's old stilts. Every other minute, he wobbled wildly as though he were going to pitch onto his button nose, but with much bending backwards and forwards, he managed to stay aloft.

"That was a swell circus," Roger Hamilton said as he and Susan left. "We'll be over tomorrow."

"Okay," the Macgregors answered, crowding around, still in costume, to see them off. Mike and Hilda both smiled.

When they were gone, Hilda said, "Nancy Welling broke her collarbone. She told me. She fell off a swing. She said it didn't hurt too much but it did hurt some. She's going to let me play with her dolls. She has a walking doll that's this big!"

She measured off the height of a three-year-old.

"That's wonderful, Hildy. Although how you managed to tell each other all that in the few seconds you saw her I wouldn't begin to try to figure out," Mother said. Then she looked at the rest of them. "That was a fine performance. Every one of you did well," she told them. "I enjoyed it from start to finish."

"Mike planned it," Jenny said. "We couldn't have done it before he came. And guess what! We made one dollar and thirty-five cents!"

"You're rich," Mother laughed. She put a hand on Mike's shoulder. "That was good organizing, Mike. I'll use you next time I need this family to get something accomplished."

"And what a ringmaster!" Dad teased. "John Ringling North will be up here after him. We'd better get him under contract."

Mike laughed. Then so did everyone else, for Fleet, his tail wagging sheepishly, came sidling up to Alec and licked his hand.

"WOW!" Mac said. "Watch out, Ferdinand. A lion is giving you a licking!"

18

Home from Far

IT WAS Friday night. Supper was over and the dishes were done. The sun was still high in the western sky and the evening was lovely and bright.

"We can go out to play, can't we, Mummy?" Mac begged.

"If you stay right in the yard," Mother replied. "Mr. Jackson is coming over to see Mike and Hildy before long."

"He's really coming to see me," Hilda bragged. "He wants to know if I'm all right. I saved one little teeny-tiny space so that he could write 'Pop' on my cast. I have thirty-two names on it. Did you have thirty-two names on your cast, Mother?"

Mother laughed and rumpled Hildy's short hair affectionately.

"Oh, I'm sure I didn't. You're the first one in this whole family to have thirty-two names on your cast, Hilda Mary," she said.

"Oh, boy!" Hilda crowed, ducking out from under Mother's hand and running outside.

They began a game of baseball. When Hilda's turn came to bat, they let her simply hold out the bat and Mike pitched at it until he hit it. Then his sister scurried to first base.

Jenny was catching. From where she crouched, she could see her parents sitting together on the veranda. They both had books open on their laps, but they had stopped reading and were watching the children play. Hilda darted back to her base with Alec in pursuit.

"You're out!" Alec shouted. "I got you, Hildy."

"You have to give me an extra chance," Hilda panted indignantly. "I've got a broken arm!"

"Hilda, get out and field," Mike told her.

"Okay, okay," she muttered darkly.

Mike grinned at Jenny as Alec picked up the bat.

"Now for my slow ball, Jenny," he said, "and watch this curve!"

Alec braced himself. He took a firmer grip on his bat. The ball flew straight across the plate at exactly the same speed as Mike's last pitch.

"Aw, you were kidding," Alec accused.

"Strike one!" Mike said cheerfully. Then he relented. "Put your bat up a bit, Alec."

Alec tried. Mike frowned. Then he put down the ball and came up behind the smaller boy.

"Like this," he said, placing Alec's hands differently on the bat and showing him where to plant his feet. "Now swing. Relax. Okay, let's try it."

The pitch came. Whack! Alec stood stock-still, astonished delight spreading over his face, as the ball sailed across the yard, bounced off the garage roof and landed smack in the peonies.

"Run, you dope. RUN!" Jenny gave him a shove.

She watched him go. Never in all her life had she felt any happier than she did right at this minute. The game, the yard spilling over with buttery sunshine, her mother nearby watching, Alec playing just like any little boy, Mike her fast friend — oh, just everything was right and good. "Michael would have liked Mike," she thought, and none of her joy faded as she thought of her twin. It was almost as if he were here, with her. She had sung his song the day before. She had worn his clown suit. They were playing a game he had loved playing, in the yard where he and she had played just the summer before.

"Mike! Hildy!" Mother called. "Here's your father."

The Jacksons deserted the game and made for the veranda.

"Hi, Pop," Hilda shouted at him even before she got there. "Look . . . look at my sling. And see, inside I have a cast, too. You can write your name right there. Just write 'Pop.' I didn't keep enough room for you to put Charlie Jackson."

Pop borrowed a pen from Dad and obediently wrote "Pop" in the small square she had saved for him. Then he sat down and took her on his knee for a minute. Hilda told him about falling, about the hospital and the X-ray, about Nancy Welling and her walking doll. She had been over to see it that afternoon.

"Say," Pop said suddenly, shifting her a little and looking at her more closely, "I think you're getting thinner."

"I am." Hilda beamed at him. "I've lost four and a half pounds. It's eating all those vegetables that does it," she added wisely.

Mike perched on the veranda railing and listened contentedly. This was the fourth time Pop had been to see them, and Hildy always talked solidly for the first ten minutes.

After the first time, Pop had been his old self again. The Macgregor children had learned to drift into the room soon after he arrived. Pop always welcomed another listener. The bigger the audience, the better the story. The younger children swallowed his tales hook, line, and sinker, but Mike and Jenny sent laughing glances back and forth when things got too wild to be believed. Once, near the end of his second visit, Pop had said suddenly, "You okay now, Mike?"

"So Dad was right. He was worried about me," Mike had thought.

Taken off guard by the question and his own thought, he had looked at the floor rather than at his father and had mumbled, "Sure, I'm fine."

"Mike," Pop said now, just as suddenly, "how about coming for a walk?"

"I thought you came to see ME!" Hilda protested as he slid her gently to the floor.

"I did," he smiled. "I did, Hildy, but I came to see Mike too. We won't be long."

Mike was surprised but proud as they set out together. Fleet was with them, of course, but this was the first time since he had come to the Macgregors that he had been alone with Pop. Even though his father seemed his old self, Mike could not forget the bothered look on his face that first time, and he had been tongue-tied with Pop in the last weeks. But now there was so much to talk about. The circus, first of all . . .

But Pop started first. "Mike, how would you like to come and live with me?" he asked. Mike stopped in his tracks and stared stupidly at the man beside him. He was so taken aback that his mouth dropped open.

"What . . . why . . . live with you!" he echoed. "How?"

"Well, I don't want you unhappy," Pop said slowly, as though, once again, he found it difficult to fit his thoughts with words. "I figured, if you wanted, I could get my landlady to put an extra cot in my room. You could sleep there. You could have your breakfast and supper there, just like I do, and I guess you could get your noon meal at a lunch counter. You'd be alone a lot because I have to work late some nights, but I want to do what is right for you. After all, you're the only son I've got. And if you're not happy . . ."

"What about Hildy?"

"It's because of her that I arranged to have you put in a foster home. She needs a woman taking care of her. She seems happy here and the Macgregors say they would hate to lose her." What had the Macgregors said about him, Mike wondered. Pop read his mind. "They like you too, Mike. Mr. Macgregor said you were one of the family already and Mrs. Macgregor agreed. But what about you? What do you want?"

Suddenly a frightening idea came into Mike's head. Maybe Pop was unhappy. Mike had visited the boardinghouse. It seemed stuffy and dull.

"Pop," he asked at last. "Are you . . . lonely? I mean would you like it better if you had me there with you?"

He was studying his feet as he asked, stepping with extreme care not to tread on one of the lines that crisscrossed the sidewalk.

Pop hesitated. In that instant's pause, Mike realized deep inside himself how much his father really loved him. He saw too that Pop had offered to take Mike to live with him because of this love, even though his life would be easier if his son went on living at the Macgregors'.

Pop belonged to a bowling league. Would he give that up so that he could come home nights to Mike? What about the times when he and a couple of his old Navy friends went off fishing or hunting and stayed away for a couple of days at a time? Mike knew how important these men were to Pop.

They had been boys together. They were familiar figures in most of Pop's tall tales. Mike remembered grown-up talk and tried to see himself and Pop talking to each other in their room in the boardinghouse. Pop could not tell stories forever. And how could he, Mike, hope to entertain him the way friends of his own age did?

"Mike, if you are unhappy, I'll be glad to take you," Pop said, determination in his voice.

Something inside Mike wanted to cry. His dream of a home with Pop, a home with just himself and Hilda and his father living together like any family, was ending.

Yet now there were Jenny and Mother and Dad. There was Fleet. How could he leave the big dog who was now looking up at him with puzzled, anxious eyes? There was Alec, who needed a big brother to teach him to play baseball. There was Mac with his goofy remarks, and there was Hilda. He knew that to Hilda he was somebody all her own, a little different from the Macgregors, a little more part of herself. Even though she had a new haircut and pretty clothes, even though she was thinner and had learned to eat most vegetables and rarely whined, even though she had Jenny to share a room with, she needed him.

And I need her, he admitted suddenly.

He needed all of them. He needed to finish learning to play chess. He needed to be part of planning other events like their circus. He had to put the roof on the playhouse. He had to be there when Dad read the rest of *Warrior Scarlet*.

"I'm not unhappy, Pop," he said, ignoring the tight feeling in his throat. "I like it at the Macgregors' now. They have kids there I can play with. They've been . . . they feel almost as though they were my family."

He looked up at Pop. He saw the relief in his father's face, but the love that he also saw there took any hurt away.

"You're still my Pop!" he said suddenly, flinging his arms around Pop's middle and feeling Pop's arms gathering him in. "You'll always be my Pop. I love you the best."

"I know that, son," Pop said. "I'm sure of that. But I'm glad you've decided to stay with them. They're nice people. I like them too. And I was worried about leaving Hildy there alone. Let's go back now, but there's no need to hurry. There's nobody I'd rather walk with."

Fleet, his eyes on Mike's face, barked sharply, anxiously. Mike laughed shakily.

"I'm okay," he said, running his hand over the setter's smooth head. Then, as father and son turned to start back, Mike added, "Come on, boy. It's time to go home."

19

With Love from Jenny

THE baseball game fell to pieces when Mike and Hilda left. The three Macgregors played catch for a while. Then Mac saw Pop leaving with Michael, and he ran off to see what Hilda wanted to do.

It was then that Jenny saw it. On a leaf, close behind her, a small golden caterpillar was taking a walk. She stood still and watched him for just a moment. Then she called softly, "Alec."

"What is it?"

She made no answer, so he came over to see.

"Don't be scared," Jenny said hurriedly, taking hold of him by one arm before he knew what was happening. "I want you to look at a bug."

Alec twisted, trying to get free, but she held fast.

"I promise I won't drop it on you or anything. It can't fly. It can't crawl fast enough to get near you unless you want it to. Just look at it. Come on, Alec."

Unwillingly, Alec peered where she pointed. Jenny's voice went on, weaving a spell which bound him there.

"See its little face. See how it nods its head. Its feelers are sort of like plumes on a hat. I like its fuzz, all yellowy. It's kind of like a pussy willow."

"Pussy willows are gray," Alec corrected her, but he had stopped struggling and started to listen.

"Alec," Jenny said, thinking fast, "do you know what a caterpillar feels like?"

At once, she saw her mistake. His face went small and tight as he remembered. He gave one great wrench and she almost lost her grip on him.

"Wait, Alec," she said hurriedly, her voice rising. "Listen for a minute. I didn't mean that. Listen!"

She jerked his arm sharply and the glazed look went out of his eyes.

"I meant . . . have you ever held a caterpillar in your hand? Do you know how one feels just in your hand?"

Jenny felt his sudden shiver, but he shook his head.

She reached out her free hand and gently pried the caterpillar off its leaf. It curled up in a ball in her palm. Alec watched, terrified but fascinated.

"It's not the way you think," Jenny declared firmly. She paused, searching for the right words. What DID he think? How could she make him understand . . . and believe?

"It's soft and dry and quiet," she mused. "It's not even moving. But when it does, it just inches along on its baby feet. You know what? . . . If you put your hand out, down near the ground, I could slide this caterpillar into your hand very carefully . . . and if it really felt awful, you could dump it onto the grass like a shot. I'll bet you'd like it if you tried it even once. I'll bet you could hold it long enough for me to count to five. I dare you, Alec. I dare you to try!"

Alec eyed the tiny caterpillar uneasily. Jenny moved her hand a little so the caterpillar wouldn't uncurl and start walking around. She felt as though Alec were a small wild animal she had caught. She was taming him by speaking quietly and moving gently.

"Okay," he agreed at last, his voice small and quavering.

They squatted down side by side. Alec held out his hand. The palm was wet with perspiration. He wiped it off hastily on the seat of his jeans and offered it again. As Jenny moved the caterpillar toward him, she could see his whole arm tremble — but he kept his hand there ready. Slowly, oh so slowly, she transferred the fuzzy little ball from her palm to his.

"One," she counted right away.

Alec stayed perfectly still. He stared down at what he held. Jenny could hear him breathing.

"Two."

"Three."

The caterpillar uncurled timidly and looked around. He was as nervous as the little boy who held him.

"Four."

"Jenny," Alec gasped, his eyes wide with excitement, "he's going to walk. He's going to walk on my hand."

"Five," Jenny said, but she knew she did not have to. Alec had no desire to drop his new friend now. Suddenly, he cupped both hands so his prize could not escape. Then he stood up and, trying not to joggle, ran for the veranda.

Mike and Pop had just come back. Mother and Dad, knowing what Pop had come to suggest, looked at Mike and tried to show on their faces how much they had come to care for him. Mike stood at the bottom of the steps, smiling back at them, feeling suddenly shy, and yet at the same time feeling as though he really belonged somewhere at last.

"Mother!" Alec shouted. "Mother! Mother!"

They all turned and watched him running toward them. Jenny, flushed with victory, was right behind him.

Alec held out his cupped hands for them all to see.

"I'm not scared," he said, his voice cracking with the wonder of it. "I'm holding a real live caterpillar. Jenny found him. I'm going to put him in a jar with holes punched in the lid and feed him and have him for a pet."

"Why, Alec, how lovely," Mother said. "I have the very jar you need."

She stood up to go and get it. For one shining instant, she and Mike and Jenny smiled at each other over Alec's bent head.